"You ought to be afraid of staying the night alone with me," Rafe said.

Sidonie laughed. "I'm not scared."

"Maybe you should be," he muttered. "I've been known to take advantage of sweet, young things."

"I'm not sweet," Sidonie said, sitting down on the edge of the bed. Then she kicked off her shoes and began rolling the leg warmer down her right leg.

"What are you doing?"

"Getting ready for bed." She took off the other leg warmer. Grabbing the hem of her sweater, she pulled it up far enough to expose her midriff.

"You won't take your clothes off in front of me."

"Oh, yes I will." Sidonie grinned before giving him a pitying look. "Give it up, McMasters. I'm staying no matter what you say."

She pulled the sweater over her head. When she could see again, the door was closing. Slowly.

"Good night, Mr. McMasters," she cooed sweetly.

Dear Reader,

Love is always in the air at Silhouette Romance. But this month, it might take a while for the characters of May's stunning lineup to figure that out! Here's what some of them have to say:

"I've just found out the birth mother of my son is back in town. What's a protective single dad to do?"—FABULOUS FATHER Jared O'Neal in Anne Peters's *My Baby, Your Son*

"What was I thinking, inviting a perfect—albeit beautiful—stranger to stay at my house?"—member of THE SINGLE DADDY CLUB, Reece Newton, from *Beauty and the Bachelor Dad* by Donna Clayton

"I've got one last chance to keep my ranch but it means agreeing to marry a man I hardly know!"—Rose Murdock from *The Rancher's Bride* by Stella Bagwell, part of her TWINS ON THE DOORSTEP miniseries

"Would you believe my little white lie of a fiancé just showed up—and he's better than I ever imagined!"—Ellen Rhoades, one of our SURPRISE BRIDES in Myrna Mackenzie's *The Secret Groom*

"I will not allow my search for a bride to be waylaid by that attractive, but totally unsuitable, redhead again!"—sexy rancher Rafe McMasters in *Cowboy Seeks Perfect Wife* by Linda Lewis

"We know Sabrina would be the perfect mom for us—we just have to convince Dad to marry her!"—the precocious twins from Gayle Kaye's *Daddyhood*

Happy Reading!

Melissa Senate
Senior Editor

Please address questions and book requests to:
Silhouette Reader Service
U.S.: 3010 Walden Ave., P.O. Box 1325, Buffalo, NY 14269
Canadian: P.O. Box 609, Fort Erie, Ont. L2A 5X3

COWBOY SEEKS PERFECT WIFE

Linda Lewis

Silhouette
R O M A N C E™
Published by Silhouette Books
America's Publisher of Contemporary Romance

For Melissa Jeglinski's mother, Delphine Jeglinski.
Because she has such a wonderful daughter, and
because she read my first book and liked it.

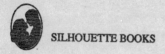 SILHOUETTE BOOKS

ISBN 0-373-19226-6

COWBOY SEEKS PERFECT WIFE

Copyright © 1997 by Linda Kay West

Books by Linda Lewis

Silhouette Romance

Honeymoon Suite #1113
The Husband Hunt #1135
Cowboy Seeks Perfect Wife #1226

LINDA LEWIS

did not begin writing until she was fifty, having frittered away her youth on law school and a career as a tax attorney. However, she did find time during those wasted years for reading, reading, reading. Romance novels are her favorite genre because the woman always wins and the books always end happily. When it was time to decide on a retirement career, writing romance novels won hands down over preparing tax returns. Fortunately, Silhouette went along with her plan and agreed to publish her books. Linda lives in New Orleans with five cats and a long-haired Chihuahua named Tupsa. Write her at P.O. Box 6098, New Orleans, Louisiana 70174.

Rancher Rafe McMasters's essential requirements for the perfect wife:

1. The perfect wife wouldn't go around giving cute little names to my livestock. Because Sidonie named my new calf "Baby," I had to change the menu for my housewarming BBQ!

2. The perfect wife wouldn't keep me awake at night with thoughts of her flaming red hair and dancer's legs. After all, I've got a ranch to run here!

3. The perfect wife would know her way around a kitchen. Sidonie might be able to heat *me* up, but a hardworking cowboy needs his meat and potatoes sometimes.

4. The perfect wife wouldn't be doing a kick line in the middle of my living room. Sidonie might call it shaping up, but if she keeps shaking her booty all over my house, *I'm* going to fall apart!

5. The perfect wife wouldn't make me fall in love with her. And I am in serious danger of falling for a certain chorus girl....

Chapter One

Sidonie Saddler slammed her foot on the brakes, and her brand-new red pickup truck shuddered to a stop. The small dog on the seat next to her slid onto the floor and looked accusingly at Sidonie.

"Sorry, pup. I wasn't expecting a gate. Are you okay?"

The solemn-faced dog hopped back onto the seat, turned around three times and curled up into a ball. Sidonie gave the animal a quick pat and opened the truck door. She eyed the shiny aluminum gate illuminated by the headlights. "There shouldn't be a gate," she muttered, wincing as she straightened her left leg to get out of the truck.

The road only led to one place, her father's ranch— her ranch for the twelve years since his death. Sidonie unfastened the gate and swung it open, then returned to the pickup and drove through. She hadn't lived in the country for years, but she remembered to stop and close the gate behind her.

"We're almost home," she told her passenger. Excitement began to build inside her, muting the painful throb from her left knee. Against doctor's orders, she'd taken the brace off for the drive from Dallas to Cache, Texas, and she'd been paying the price since Alvarado. Ignoring the pain, Sidonie wondered at her strong feeling of homecoming. She'd always thought of herself as a gypsy wanderer, a rolling stone, not a homebody.

Lately, though, even before the accident, she'd begun having these strange longings for home and hearth. At first she'd shrugged them off and gone on to the next rehearsal, the next opening with her usual enthusiasm for the new and different. New people and different places had always been the lure that kept her moving on, never settling down.

But a new kind of excitement gripped her now, and the feeling had grown with every mile. She was going *home*. Embarrassing to admit, but the sound of the pickup's wheels on the paved road sounded suspiciously like Dorothy's voice in *The Wizard of Oz*. She could swear the tires were humming, "There's no place like home, no place like home."

But Cache, Texas, hadn't been her home for years. Not since she was five. She hadn't visited the place more than two or three times since Buck died. She hadn't gotten emotional on those trips, so why this time?

After a few moments she figured it out. Sanctuary. She was heading for sanctuary. The ranch was going to be her refuge while she healed and regained her strength. This feeling of homecoming wouldn't last. As soon as her body was well and strong again the old restlessness would return and she'd be on her way again.

But when she caught her first glimpse of the frame house with its wraparound porches, Sidonie had to swallow a lump the size of a grapefruit. Blinking tears away, she patted the little dog on the head. "Home, sweet home," she murmured, a little embarrassed by her weepy sentimentality.

She sat for a few moments drinking in the moonlit scene. The hackberry tree she'd first climbed when she was eight stood on the side of the house, one of its branches still drooping temptingly close to Sidonie's bedroom window. Crepe myrtle trees her mother had planted flanked the short walk to the front porch, and pecan trees towered over the back of the house. "Everything is just the same." Sidonie sighed, relieved. She hadn't known until that moment how much she longed for something familiar, something unchanging.

"Enough being maudlin," she said briskly, blinking the mist from her eyes. It wasn't like her to get emotional over a place, even the place where she'd been born.

Sidonie opened the truck door and got out, waiting until the dog had jumped to the ground before starting up the walk. Wagging its tail, the little dog followed her to the front porch.

The porch light was on, thank goodness. When she'd called Judge Longstreet to have the water and electricity turned on, she'd only talked to his answering machine. The welcoming light proved he'd gotten the message. It had occurred to her, on the long drive from Dallas, that it might take more than a few hours to get the job done. The thought of arriving at a cold, dark house in the middle of the night had almost made her stop at the next motel and wait until morning to finish the drive. That would have been the sensible thing to do.

Sidonie reached down and scratched the scruffy little dog behind her ears. "But if I'd done the sensible thing, I wouldn't have met you."

Remembering how the dog had been cowering under a picnic bench at the rest area where she'd stopped to stretch her legs, she had to blink away more tears. Poor little thing, so lost and alone. She'd lured the abandoned and starving dog to her with cold French fries left over from a stop at a Dairy Queen.

"Come on, dog, let's get in out of the cold."

The porch light went off the instant Sidonie put her key in the lock. The small hairs on the back of her neck rose as the door swung open before she turned the key. Someone was in the house! Sidonie's brain barely registered the dark, masculine shape in the shadowed doorway before she reacted instinctively.

She kneed the man in the groin.

Unfortunately she used her injured knee to do it. The man fell to the floor and folded into a fetal position. Sidonie fell on top of him, clutching her knee. He did not break her fall—the man was as hard as the hardwood floor.

"Oh! Oh! Oh!" moaned Sidonie.

"Ow! Ow! Ow!" groaned the man.

The dog seemed to think it was a game. She was dancing around, yapping at the two entangled humans.

The man shoved Sidonie aside and rolled onto his knees. After a few deep breaths, he got up. Bent over, he staggered to the wall switch and turned on the hall light.

"Why did you do that?" he snarled. "Who the hell are you?"

"Who the hell wants to know?" Sidonie snarled back as she struggled to a sitting position. That was as far as she could get by herself.

She eyed the man leaning against the wall, gasping for breath. He didn't look like a burglar. More like a banker—if bankers ever had a sleepy, rumpled sort of look. He was wearing a white shirt, unbuttoned and untucked in, and dark blue trousers. A conservatively striped red-and-navy silk tie hung loosely around his neck.

The clincher was his feet. They were bare. No shoes, no socks. He couldn't be a burglar. Everyone knew burglars wore black, from their ski masks to their rubber-soled shoes.

"Why did you knee me?" he asked again, through tightly clenched teeth.

"I didn't expect anyone to be in my house. Why are you here?"

"I live here."

"No, you don't." She held out her hand. "Help me up."

"Yes, ma'am, at your service, ma'am," he said, hobbling closer. His overly polite response did not sound completely sincere to Sidonie, but she took his hand, anyway.

The man yanked her upright before she was ready to stand. Her knee promptly buckled, and Sidonie fell into the man's arms. Holding on for dear life, she couldn't help but notice that he wasn't a flabby kind of banker. Solid as a rock. Sidonie looked into the man's dark brown eyes. An involuntary shiver ran down her spine. This man might not be a burglar, but that didn't mean he wasn't dangerous.

"What did you say your name was?"

"McMasters. Rafe McMasters," he muttered, trying to unwind Sidonie's arms from around his neck.

"Don't let me go! I'll fall."

He let her go, and she promptly fell at his feet. Or would have if he hadn't grabbed her around the waist at the last minute.

"What's wrong with you, Miss...?"

"Sidonie...Saddler," she gasped, gritting her teeth against the pain. "Nothing's wrong with me. I have a little problem with my knee, but it's only temporary."

"I have a problem with your knee, too," he said. "I sure as hell hope it's only temporary. Wait a minute. Did you say Saddler? You're Buck Saddler's daughter?"

Sidonie immediately felt safer, and not because McMasters still had his arms around her waist. If the man had known her father, he couldn't be too dangerous.

Before she could do more than nod, McMasters swung her into his arms and carried her into the parlor. Setting her down on the couch, he asked, "What are you doing here?"

Sidonie stuck her nose in the air, partly to convey a haughty attitude and partly to cover her confusion. Dozens of men—most of them dance partners—had swung her into their arms. But none of them had affected her as this man had done. With only a touch, and an impersonal one at that, he had her heart pounding and her palms sweating. She eyed him suspiciously. He still looked like a banker. It couldn't be him making her feel all hot and bothered. The strange weakness she'd felt in his arms must be a side effect of her medication. Except she hadn't had a pill all day.

"Well? Are you going to answer me?"

Her chin came up another notch. "Here happens to be my home."

"Not now it isn't. And not for another three months. I lease this place."

"Oh, no, you don't. The land maybe, but not the house. I never lease the house. Judge Longstreet wouldn't do that without telling—" Sidonie stopped.

She hadn't actually read the last lease the judge had sent her, but the cover letter had mentioned something about new terms. "Uh-oh. We may have a problem." She reached down and rubbed her knee. "Would you mind getting my knee brace out of the pickup?"

He started for the door.

"My suitcase, too, please and thank you."

He paused and looked over his shoulder, frowning. "You won't be needing that. You're not staying." He turned away and walked out the door.

"My pain medicine is in the suitcase," she called after him.

While she waited for his return, Sidonie shrugged out of her black leather trench coat. She was wearing a pale pink angora sweater with cherry red skorts and pink leg warmers. Sidonie loved pink and red, and she didn't care a fig what the world thought about redheads who wore clashing colors.

And she didn't care what McMasters said about a lease. She was staying in her house. If anyone was leaving, he was. She'd evict him. Judge Longstreet would tell her how to go about it. Satisfied that it was only a matter of time before she had her house to herself, Sidonie stood up. She was bent at the waist, touching her toes, when McMasters returned, carrying her brace in one hand and her battered suitcase in the other.

She straightened up and reached for the ceiling, stretching first her left, then her right side. When McMasters caught sight of her, he stopped in his tracks and gaped. Sidonie sighed. She often had that effect on men. She attributed it to her spectacular body and her flame red hair. Males, she had learned, were often impressed by such superficialities.

While he stood staring at her with his mouth open, she looked him over, but more discreetly. She, having a dancer's appreciation for a beautiful body, could admire his tall, rangy frame without ogling. His face wasn't bad, either—if a square jaw, bold cheekbones and a sensuous mouth appealed.

She took her suitcase from him, being careful to avoid touching him. She was almost sure it hadn't been his touch that had caused her pulse to race, but she wasn't taking any chances. Not while she was tired and coping with her bewildering feelings of homecoming.

McMasters closed his mouth, narrowed his eyes and gave her another look she recognized. Pure, unadulterated desire. Tiny chills skittered down her spine, and she could hear her pulse pounding in her ears. If he was exhibiting the signs of instant lust, maybe what she was feeling was the same thing. Several seconds ticked by as they looked at each other.

With an effort, Sidonie tore her gaze from his hypnotic stare and set the suitcase down and opened it. She couldn't want a man she'd just met. She didn't have time for lust, if that truly was what she was feeling. Rummaging through the case, she located her bottle of pain pills. She held it up with a triumphant grin. "Thanks, I needed this."

"Do you want a glass of water?" he asked, frowning at her.

Maybe she'd misread him, too. At second glance, he looked more aggravated than attracted. "That would be nice."

He left the room and returned in a few minutes with the water. As he handed it to her, he glanced at the open suitcase at her feet.

"Is this all you brought with you?"

"Yes." That was all she owned, besides her temporary investment in the pickup. Sidonie prided herself on being able to carry all her worldly possessions in one suitcase.

"Good. You're not planning on a long stay."

"Just long enough for my knee to heal. A few weeks, a couple of months at most."

"You won't have any trouble finding a room to rent somewhere. For the rest of tonight, you can go to the motel over on Highway 283." He came closer and handed her the molded plastic brace. "Close the gate on your way out."

"I closed the gate on my way in. Why is there a gate? The road doesn't go anywhere but here."

"Now it goes to my place, too, and I put up the gate so the road wouldn't become public property. I like my privacy. So feel free to leave, the sooner the better."

Sidonie fitted the brace on her leg and fastened the Velcro straps. "I'm staying in my house. In my room," she said firmly. "That's not negotiable."

He crossed his arms, calling Sidonie's attention to his broad chest. "Everything's negotiable, Miss Saddler,'' he drawled. ''But I can tell you right now, you're not staying here.''

''Why not?''

McMasters clenched his square jaw. ''I have a lease.''

''So you say,'' Sidonie rejoined coolly. ''May I see it?'' She could tell that request knocked him off balance. Sidonie smiled seductively, intending to keep him that way.

He shook his head. ''Not tonight. The lease is at the bank, in my safety-deposit box.''

''Tomorrow, then. But until you can prove you belong here, I'm staying.'' She reached for her suitcase and started for her bedroom at the rear of the house. ''You can stay, too, of course. I wouldn't dream of making you go to a motel at this time of night.''

Making a choking sound, he moved in front of her, blocking her exit from the parlor. ''I was here first,'' he said, snapping his dark brows together in a menacing scowl.

It didn't scare her. She was not in the mood to be intimidated by a...banker. ''Not really. I was born here.'' She squeezed by him.

He sucked in his breath as she brushed against him. Sidonie turned her head away, to hide her smug smile. There was more than one way to handle a man, especially the pompous kind, but this way worked so well.

He let her pass, then followed her so closely Sidonie could feel his hot breath on the back of her neck. She walked faster, not caring that speed accentuated her ungainliness.

''What kind of female are you, anyway? You ought to be afraid of staying the night alone with me.''

Sidonie laughed. She wasn't falling for his dangerous man act. "I'm not scared."

"Maybe you should be," he growled. "I've been known to take advantage of sweet young things."

"I'm not so sweet," she countered.

"Not that young, either."

She stopped in her tracks. "There's no need to be insulting." Twenty-eight wasn't old, even for a dancer. She still had a few good years left, provided her knee cooperated.

"I don't suppose you're worried about your reputation, either." He put his hands on her shoulders.

Sidonie jumped. She could handle him fine, as long as he didn't touch her. She tried to shrug out from under his hands, but he only tightened his grip. "What does that mean?"

"A lady would worry about what people will say when they find out she spent the night with me."

Sidonie tossed her head, sending her red hair flying. "Would she, really? Is spending the night with a banker considered unladylike in this part of the world?"

"I'm not a banker," he said, taking his hands away. He sounded startled.

At the door to her old bedroom, Sidonie turned to face him. "No? A preacher, then?"

"Hell, no."

She waited. Apparently he wasn't going to elaborate. "I'm a dancer. And you might as well know—I don't care what people say about me."

"I didn't think so. But I do care what people say about me. You can't stay here."

Sidonie arched an eyebrow. "Why?"

He rolled his eyes back. "I have a lease."

"And now you have a roommate to go with it."

"I don't want a roommate! The lease—which you signed—entitles me to exclusive possession of this house for three more months."

"You don't have to stay. I won't sue you if you break the lease."

A muscle worked in his jaw. "I'm staying. You're leaving."

"No, I'm not. Get used to it, McMasters. And don't worry. Like I told you before, I don't care what people will say."

"No, you wouldn't, would you? Your type isn't bothered by gossip," he said, sneering.

"My type? Golly, gee whiz. You must be one of those old fogies who think show business isn't respectable. I've heard about your kind. Repressed, inhibited—"

He reached for her.

"Hey!" Sidonie slapped his hands away. "What do you think you're doing?"

"First I'm going to shut you up. Then I'm throwing you out."

"You can't do that." Sidonie backed into her room. "I need to stay here. I don't have anyplace else to go."

"The motel," he said, advancing toward her.

"I took a pain pill, remember?" She whimpered, shooting him her best pitiful look. "Once it kicks in, I won't be able to drive."

"Not a problem. I'll drive you there."

She glared at him. So much for appealing to his sensitive side. The man was a cold, unfeeling clod. And a sanctimonious snob, to boot. How could she ever have thought he was attractive? "I'm not going to a motel, especially not a tacky no-tell motel like the one on 283. This is my home, and I'm staying right here, lease or no lease."

"Don't try to con me, Miss Saddler. You may own this place, but it's not your home. You haven't lived here since you were five years old."

"I beg your pardon. I'll have you know I spent every summer here until Daddy—until I was sixteen. And I've been back to visit a few times since then, when I was between jobs."

He was not impressed. She could tell by the way he continued to look at her as if she were the poster girl for tacky behavior.

Narrowing her eyes, she tried another angle. "Look, Mr. McMasters. I can't go anyplace else. I don't have any money. Medical bills, you know?" She pointed to her knee. "Plus, I used the last of my ready cash to buy a pickup."

"I'll advance you next month's rent."

Exasperated, Sidonie threw up her hands and turned her back to him. She wasn't getting anywhere with the arrogant, stubborn son of— "Oh, look. Isn't that cute?"

With a triumphant grin, Sidonie pointed to the dog curled up in a ball in the middle of her white four-poster bed. "We can't go to a motel. They don't allow pets. Where are the sheets? As soon as I make up the bed and take a quick shower, I'll—"

"The dog can stay. You can pick her up tomorrow. What's her name?"

"I don't know. We just met. Go away, McMasters. I'm tired, and I want to go to bed." Sidonie sat on the edge of the bed and unfastened the brace. Then she

kicked off her shoes and began rolling the leg warmer
down her right leg.

"You ought to give the dog a name if you plan on
keeping her." His gaze shifted from the dog to her.
"What are you doing?"

"Getting ready for bed." She took off the other leg
warmer, revealing a tiny scar on her left knee. Grabbing the hem of her sweater, she pulled it up far
enough to expose her midriff.

"You won't take your clothes off in front of me."

"Oh, yes, I will." Sidonie grinned. Modesty was
one virtue a dancer lost early. She'd undressed onstage, offstage and backstage, in crowded, communal
dressing rooms for years. She gave him a pitying look.
"Give it up, McMasters. Me and the no-name dog are
staying."

She pulled the sweater over her head. When she
could see again, the door was closing. Slowly.

"Good night, Mr. McMasters," she cooed sweetly.

The door opened a crack and she could see one eye
flashing balefully. "All right! One night. You can stay
here one night. But that's it. Tomorrow you're finding
someplace else. Understand?"

"You don't have to shout," she yelled.

"I never shout," he yelled back, slamming the door
shut.

Rafe stared at the bedroom door he'd run for, the
minute Sidonie started her striptease. Except she
hadn't been teasing. She'd been playing to win, and
she had succeeded. She was sleeping in his house.
Only for one night, sure, but that was bound to be one
night too many. If anyone found out, and odds were
that someone would, the good people of Proffit County

would have a new episode to add to the saga of Rafe McMasters. They'd talk and talk about him and the redheaded temptress who now sat triumphantly behind the closed bedroom door.

They'd think he hadn't changed at all.

Tugging his tie from around his neck, Rafe paused at the door to his room. He'd been getting ready for bed himself when he'd heard someone drive up. He glanced at his watch. That was only half an hour ago. He'd been tired, ready for sleep, until she'd shown up and attacked him.

Now he was wide-awake. With a disgusted groan he turned on his bare heel and walked through the house to the front room. Heading for the window, he pulled the curtains back and looked up the hill opposite the house. He could see the dark outline of *his* house silhouetted against the night sky.

A fierce sense of pride filled him. He'd done it! It had taken fifteen long years, countless hours of hard work and a little luck, but he was finally back where he belonged. The land had been the first step. No one in his family had ever owned his own land. Beginning with his great-grandfather, the first McMasters to settle in Proffit County, the men in his family had worked for other men all their lives. Rafe had vowed to change that, and he was well on his way to succeeding.

Over the years he'd bought the land, a few acres at a time. Now he owned a good part of the county— enough land to challenge Emmet Clancy for the title of biggest rancher in the area. But that was only the first step in executing his lifelong plan. Rafe glanced at his house on the hill again. In a few months he'd be living in the biggest and best house in the county.

After that he needed only one thing to reach his goal. A wife.

For years Rafe had planned on becoming a rancher, a respected member of the community, marrying a woman who knew what it meant to be a rancher's wife. He'd almost realized his goal years ago, when Cathy Sue Clancy had agreed to marry him, but then—

With a muttered oath Rafe stopped that line of thought. No guilt, no regrets. He'd find another woman, someone with the all the right qualities. Together they would raise a family and build a solid, respectable life together. His mouth curved in a sardonic smile. He could kiss that part of his plan goodbye, unless he could get Sidonie out of the house, and fast. No self-respecting woman—no lady—would keep company with a man living with a chorus girl.

He knew all about Sidonie. People still talked about her and her mother, the Las Vegas showgirl Buck had married thirty years ago. Almost as much as they talked about him.

Sidonie could call herself a dancer all she wanted to, but he knew darn well she only danced in the chorus. That made her a chorus girl. A tightening in his loins forced him to admit Sidonie was well endowed with all the talent needed for that job—long legs, sensuous curves and clear blue eyes filled with seductive promises. If he wasn't looking to settle down, she'd be exactly the kind of woman he'd enjoy getting to know—in the Biblical sense. But he'd sown all his wild oats years ago. No more flings for him, no matter how tempting his unwelcome guest.

Even if his feet weren't firmly set on the road to respectability, a man would think twice before getting involved with someone like Sidonie. Look what a dancing girl had done to Buck Saddler. Broken his heart, that's what. After only a few years of being a rancher's wife, Belle had left him for the bright lights of Broadway, taking Sidonie with her. After that, they hadn't stayed put in any one place for long.

Buck had shown him postcards and playbills from every major and not so major American city, and more than a few European ones. Belle and Sidonie had traveled all over the world. Rafe suppressed the sudden twinge of envy caused by visions of London and Paris. Looking up the hill at his house, he concentrated hard on why he'd come back to Proffit County. He'd seen some of the world himself—mostly corporate boardrooms and luxury hotels, now that he thought about it. But there would be time to travel again, once he had his plan fully realized.

First he had to get rid of Sidonie.

His reputation would have sent any other female running for cover, but Sidonie obviously didn't know anything about him. The one time his notoriety might have been of some use, he had to come up against a woman who'd never heard the stories about his wild and woolly youth. She hadn't run. She'd kneed him.

He should have grabbed her by the scruff of her shapely neck and thrown her out the door. He would have, too, if her surprise attack hadn't taken him out of the match.

By the time he'd recovered, his brain had registered several important facts about her. One, Sidonie Saddler was the daughter of the best friend he'd ever had in Proffit County. Two, she was injured.

And three, she could give a ninety-year-old eunuch erotic dreams.

Chapter Two

Sidonie was awakened by a cold nose and a whine. She got up and let the dog out the front door, then looked for her reluctant host. Rafe McMasters was nowhere to be found but he'd left an envelope addressed to her on the kitchen table. It contained a check for a thousand dollars and a brief note. "Happy house hunting." He'd signed it "McMasters."

Sidonie tore up the note, but she folded the check and put it in her handbag. Lease money went to Judge Longstreet for deposit into her trust account. After she fed the dog a can of chili she found in the pantry, Sidonie returned to her bedroom.

Her single suitcase rule didn't allow for many clothes, so her wardrobe consisted mostly of rehearsal outfits—leotards, tights, shorts and slacks. She unpacked, hanging her colorful clothes—she favored primary colors over pastels—in her old closet. While stashing her underwear in the dresser, she found several pairs of faded jeans folded in the bottom drawer, along with a couple of Western shirts. Neither her old clothes nor her current wardrobe coordinated with the black plastic brace.

The brace was standing in the corner of her bedroom. She left it there. She had to go to town, and she couldn't wear the hateful thing when she drove. She topped a chrome yellow leotard and matching tights with a turquoise wraparound skirt that ended a few inches above her knees. As soon as she'd dressed, she returned to the kitchen.

"Come on, pup." The small dog licked the last of the chili from its mouth and followed Sidonie to the pickup.

Once they were on their way, Sidonie looked at the dog. "The fuddy-duddy was right about one thing. You need a name." Scratching the dog behind the ear, she thought for a moment. "Gypsy. You're a gypsy, like me. That's what I'll call you."

She dropped Gypsy off at the vet's, then headed for the Proffit County Courthouse and Judge Tyler Longstreet's courtroom.

"Well, well, well, aren't you a sight for sore eyes!" Judge Longstreet enveloped Sidonie in a bear hug and led her into his chambers. "When you walked in, all bright and shiny like a new penny, I couldn't believe it. You're really here." He hugged her again, then held her away from him. "How's the knee?"

"Getting better."

"When did you get in? Did you get my message?"

"Late last night. What message?"

"I called the hotel to tell you not to go home. You have a tenant, remember? Where did you stay last night? With Maggie and the doc?"

"No. I haven't seen Maggie yet. *Tenant.* That's

what I want to talk to you about, Judge.'' She paused for dramatic effect. ''There's a man in my house.''

''I know that. Isn't that what we've been talking about? Your tenant, Rafe McMasters. He leased the place a few months back.''

''I only lease the land.''

''You didn't read the last lease before you signed it, did you?'' He shook his head. ''Sidonie, girl, how many times have I told you—''

''Always read before you sign. I know. But the leases have always been the same, up until this one. Why did you lease the house?''

''Didn't you see the rent he's paying? Your trust account is pretty healthy, even after taking out that chunk for your medical bills, but you can't touch the principal until you're thirty. Not for everyday living expenses, only for emergencies. You won't be thirty for two more years. You're going to need that extra money for food and rent and other necessities, while you figure out a new way to earn a living.''

''I'll earn a living the same way I always have— dancing.''

The judge frowned. ''Not according to what the doctors told me. They said—''

''Never mind what they said. I know more about what my body can do than any doctor. I'm going to be fine. All I need is a place to relax and time to get back in shape.''

Tyler looked like he wanted to argue with her, but instead he asked, ''Where did you stay last night? You never said.''

''I stayed at home, but I had to fight that man tooth and nail to do it. He's the most—''

The judge's mouth dropped open. ''You stayed the

night with Rafe McMasters? You got into a fight with him?"

"I never laid a hand on him." A knee but not a hand. Judge Longstreet didn't need to know about that. "What's wrong? You look shocked."

"I'm not shocked. Surprised, maybe. You...and Rafe McMasters. Oh, my."

He still looked shocked to Sidonie. "Oh, for heaven's sake, Judge. Believe me, we didn't make mad, passionate love on the kitchen table."

"I didn't think you did. I know you and Rafe wouldn't..."

He looked embarrassed. Sidonie grinned. The judge had always been more naive than a man his age, in his profession, should be. "You're right about that. We definitely wouldn't. He's not my type." She wasn't sure what her type was, but arrogant, self-righteous fuddy-duddies didn't even make it to the bottom of her list. Not even if they had bodies to die for.

Judge Longstreet's bushy white eyebrows came together in a puzzled frown. Clearing his throat, he continued. "Harrumph. I'd have thought a wealthy, handsome man was almost any woman's type." His brow smoothed. "But you're smarter than most women, aren't you? What have you learned about McMasters?"

"That he's living in my house and he looks down his nose at dancers. What else should I know about him?"

The judge shot her a disappointed look. "That's all?"

Rafe had put every nerve ending she had on red alert every time he'd touched her, but she wasn't going to tell that to Judge Longstreet. She shook her head.

"Nothing else? Too bad. Rafe McMasters's homecoming has been the main topic of conversation around here for weeks. Of course, now that you've shown up, there will be something new to talk about. But the two of you together—oh, my. Him, the prodigal son come home, and you, looking just like your mother. All big, blue eyes and long, long legs...." Tyler's eyes glazed over momentarily, then he caught himself. "Harrumph. That is to say, you two will be a major topic of conversation around these parts."

"That's what he said. But why?"

"He left town under something of a cloud fifteen years ago. No one's heard from him since. Then he turns up out of the blue three months ago, holding title to half the county. Turns out he'd been buying up land here in Proffit County for years, through a nominee. But we still don't know where he was all those years, or what he's been up to."

"Okay, I can see how people might find that a little bit interesting, but why would they talk about me?"

"You know how the town's always been fascinated by your mother and you. You two are the only show business folks ever to come from Cache."

"We're not exactly famous, either one of us. Mom never made it out of the chorus line until she gave up dancing and became a choreographer. Neither have I."

"You're the closest thing to famous around these parts. Especially after that video you were in with that rock star—what's his name?"

"Duke Devlin. I do well enough for my purposes, but I'm a long way from being a star." Sidonie shrugged. "But if people find me and the stuffed shirt fascinating, they can talk about us all they want."

"Stuffed shirt? That's how you see him?"

She nodded warily. "Don't you?"

"Not hardly. Rafe McMasters was the roughest, toughest cowboy in Proffit County when he was a young man. Doing real well on the rodeo circuit, he was. But he was always in trouble, right up to and including the day he left town. Now he's back, throwing money around like it was water. How did he make his fortune? Answer me that, if you can."

Ignoring the question, which was obviously rhetorical, Sidonie concentrated on the image the judge's words conjured up—Rafe McMasters in tight jeans and cowboy boots, a Western shirt straining to cover his muscled chest.... Sidonie blinked and the image was gone.

"Cowboy? Rough and tough? You can't mean Mr. Prude and Prejudice. Judge, the man wears a three-piece suit to bed. Did you say he left town under a cloud? What on earth did he do?"

"Never you mind. You get out of here and find a place to stay. I'd let you stay with me, but a pretty young thing like you living with an old bachelor like me would cause tongues to wag, too. Why don't you go see the widow Harris? She runs a real respectable boardinghouse."

"I'm beginning to remember why Mom left here. She always told me people in Cache were much too concerned with everyone else's business." Sidonie walked around the desk and placed a kiss on the judge's receding hairline. "I'm staying at my place."

"You can't stay there. Not as long as Rafe is in residence."

"That's what I wanted to talk to you about. How do we get him out of my house?"

"He'll be out in three months. That's when the lease is up."

"Can't we break it, somehow?"

"I drew it up. You signed it. It's unbreakable."

Sidonie left the judge's chambers dismayed, but far from discouraged. She'd find a way to stay on her land, in her house, and she knew just who to go to for help. She drove to the home of her best friend in Cache, Maggie Malone Parker.

"Sidonie!" Maggie hugged her so hard she thought her ribs might snap. "When did you get here? I thought you weren't coming for another week or two. Your medical files haven't even gotten here yet."

"I broke out of the rehab center. I couldn't take it any longer. I wanted to come home." Sidonie swallowed the lump in her throat and hugged Maggie back.

Holding her friend at arm's length, she gave her a searching look. Maggie Parker was a petite...blonde. This week. She had a habit of changing her hair color every few months. Maggie claimed it was the only adventurous thing she ever did, but Sidonie knew better. They'd always been equally talented when it came to cooking up schemes.

"Aren't you supposed to be wearing a brace? And should you be driving? Where did you get that cute little truck?"

Laughing, Sidonie let Maggie lead her into the cozy cottage. "Yes, probably not and Dallas. I went straight from the airport to the dealership."

"You bought it? Does that mean you're home for good?"

"No. No." Sidonie frowned. Trust Maggie to figure out right away that it didn't make sense for her to buy a pickup. Once she had a job and was back on the road again, she'd have to sell it. "I know I should have rented a car, but I wasn't sure how long I'd be here. And I thought I'd stay in Texas for a while—there are lots of opportunities for dancers, at least in the summer. The State Fair musicals, Casa Mañana in Fort Worth...." She trailed off. She'd always been able to read Maggie like a book. Now she was reading disbelief. "I *am* going to dance again, Maggie," Sidonie said softly.

Another fierce hug. "Of course you are, sweetie. When did you get in? Just now?"

"No, late last night."

Confusion showed on Maggie's face. "Last night? Where did you stay? Not at that tacky motel at the edge of town."

She shook her head. "At home, of course."

Maggie's eyes widened. "You spent the night with Rafe McMasters?"

"Good grief! Does the whole town know he's living in my house?"

Nodding her head vigorously, Maggie pushed Sidonie in the direction of the kitchen. "Yes, indeed. Everyone knows Rafe is staying at the Saddler home place. You spent the night with him?"

"You make it sound like we slept together. We weren't even in the same room, Maggie. Only under the same roof."

Maggie had the grace to blush. "Well, of course you didn't sleep with him. You just met. But you've got to tell me everything. Where's he been all these years? Why did he come back, do you know?" Maggie was practically drooling.

"I have no idea. We spent our time together exchanging insults, not life stories," Sidonie said dryly.

"First Judge Longstreet and now you. What is so intriguing about Rafe McMasters and his homecoming?"

Maggie sighed. "I've heard stories about him ever since I was knee-high to a grasshopper. The man's a legend. But no one's seen or heard from him for fifteen years—not since he jilted Cathy Sue and ran off with that exotic dancer."

Sidonie's jaw dropped. "A stripper? He ran off with a stripper?"

"Practically left poor Cathy Sue waiting at the altar. Although I shouldn't call her poor. Her daddy's the richest man in Proffit County. Or he was, until Rafe came back. Folks are saying he's got more money than Emmet Clancy ever thought about."

"I don't know who or what you're talking about."

"No, that's right, you wouldn't. Cathy and Rafe were in high school together—eight or nine years ahead of us. It started out as a real romantic love story—Cathy Sue, the daughter of the biggest rancher in the county, and Rafe, the son of one of his cowhands. Rafe wasn't a hand, though. He was on his way to being a championship rodeo cowboy. That's when Cathy Sue and he got together."

Maggie sighed dreamily. "For a while, it looked like they would live happily ever after. Mr. Clancy eventually came around and gave his blessing to the engagement. A big church wedding was in the works—I know because one of my cousins was going to be a bridesmaid. And then, boom, it was all over. Rafe left town and never came back."

"With a stripper?"

"Well, that part of the story's a little fuzzy. Some of the men in town saw Rafe a few months later in a

honky-tonk in Fort Worth. He was with a woman a
few of them claimed they'd seen a whole lot of—
although, when push came to shove, none of them
would actually admit they'd been to a burlesque
show.''

"I don't think it's true. I can't see him running off
with a dancer.''

"Why not?''

"The way he looked at me after I told him I dance
for a living—like I just crawled out from under a
rock.''

"Get out of here! I never saw a man look at you
with anything but lusty admiration.''

"Well, Rafe McMasters does not admire me, and
the feeling is mutual. I still don't see why Rafe's a
legend if all he did was break up with his girlfriend.
Did Cathy Sue go into a decline and die of a broken
heart?''

"Not hardly. Getting jilted by Rafe was the only
bad thing that ever happened to Cathy Sue, and she
recovered from that blow pretty fast. She married her
dad's foreman—J. D. Nicholls—a few months later.''

"Well then, how did he get his reputation?''

"Rafe McMasters is a mystery. If he was fooling
around with the exotic dancer, where did he meet her?
He'd been in Cache for months, recovering from an
injury. If he wasn't cheating on Cathy Sue, why did
he leave her? She never would say. Our sweet Cathy
Sue's too much of a lady to air her dirty linen in public.''

"Do I detect a hint of sarcasm? Don't you like
Cathy Sue?''

"Not much. She's always been there for me and
every other female in Proffit County to compare our-

selves to—the ideal Texas lady, a cross between a Southern belle and a pioneer woman. Trust me, we all suffer by comparison.''

Chuckling, Sidonie asked, ''And just what makes her so special?''

''Everyone thinks Cathy Sue is the ideal home-maker, the perfect wife and mother—with the possible exception of J.D. and Darcy, her husband and daughter. They are the ones who actually have to live up to her impossibly high standards. I swear, living in the same town with her is like living next door to Martha Stewart.''

''Now, that is interesting. Why would Rafe dump someone like her? Based on our brief time together, I'd say a female paragon is exactly his type.'' Why that should give Sidonie a sinking feeling in the pit of her stomach, she couldn't begin to fathom. She sniffed dismissively. ''Too bad she's married. If she were still available, they could reconcile. Then he could move in with her and leave my house to me.''

''Some folks do think Cathy Sue is the reason he's come back. Including Cathy Sue, for one. Oh, she doesn't say so, just gets a wistful, faraway look in her eyes whenever his name is mentioned. J.D.'s not too happy, either. Probably afraid he's not up to the competition if Rafe really does make a play for his wife. After all, Rafe has his own ranch now, the biggest in the county from what I hear. J.D.'s still only the foreman at the Clancy spread. I have a feeling that if he wanted to, Rafe could get Cathy Sue with one crook of his little finger.''

''He wouldn't do that.'' Somehow she'd gotten the definite impression that, no matter how stuffy he was,

Rafe McMasters was an honorable man. Not the kind to chase after a married woman.

"You're probably right. I doubt Rafe has suddenly decided he made a mistake all those years ago. He'll find someone else to marry."

"What makes you think he's going to marry anyone?"

"That huge house he's building. It's much too big for one man. He must be planning on starting a family. Wouldn't it be great if he found a woman even more perfect than Cathy Sue? It would be refreshing to see the blue ribbons at the Proffit County Fair on something she didn't make."

"Cathy Sue beats out your peach cobbler?"

Maggie nodded. "Every damn year."

Sidonie patted Maggie on the shoulder. "All right. Here's the plan. We'll shoot her. Where does this Cathy Sue person live?"

Maggie giggled. "That's going too far, even for us. And I have to admit, the talk about him and Cathy Sue is pure speculation. And that's only one story. Some folks think he's back to get even with J.D., the theory being that if J.D. hadn't snapped Cathy Sue up so fast, she would have waited for Rafe. Other people think Rafe wants to ruin Emmet."

"Why would he want to do that?"

"All kinds of reasons, most of which are kind of vague. He's a real mystery."

"Well, someone else can solve him. I've got other things to do. Like hug my goddaughter. Where is she?"

"Elizabeth's at school of course. She's so excited about you coming home. She's discovered ballet on the learning channel and she wants dance lessons."

Sidonie frowned. Dance lessons? Maggie knew Sidonie's feelings about teaching—that was what dancers did after they retired. Was Maggie pushing her toward a new career, too? "The closest dance studio is in Dallas, isn't it?"

Maggie didn't pursue the subject. "Where are you going to live until Rafe moves out? I'd offer to let you stay here, but we only have the two bedrooms, now that Rayburn's turned one into a study."

"I have a place to stay. Unfortunately I'll have to share it with McMasters. It turns out he really does have a lease on the house, and Judge Longstreet says I can't get out of it."

Maggie shot her a dubious look. "Do you think he'll go for a roommate?"

"Not willingly. That's why I came to you. We have to figure out a way to make him go for it. You always were good at getting people to do what you wanted."

Maggie grinned. "Don't let Rayburn hear you say that—I've got him convinced he's the boss."

Crossing her heart, Sidonie grinned back. "My lips are sealed."

Maggie's brows drew together in fierce concentration. "There was something...I know! I saw it in the paper just this morning. He's advertised for a live-in cook/housekeeper. But I'm pretty sure he means for the house he's building. It won't be finished for another month or so." She rummaged around in a stack of magazines and pulled out the latest copy of the *Cache Register*, the town's weekly newspaper.

Sidonie snatched it out of her hands. "Let me see that." Turning to the classified ads at the back of the paper, she quickly ran her eye down the columns. "Aha! You're right, Maggie. Here it is." She scanned the ad. "This is perfect. I won't even try to talk him into letting me stay. I'll just apply for the job. I'd have to clean and cook for myself, anyway."

"Don't count your chickens before they're hatched, Sidonie. Every woman in town under eighty is going to apply for that job."

"But I've got the inside track. My suitcase is already unpacked. And the ad does say to start in two months. I'll just have to convince him he needs a housekeeper now."

"Well, maybe that will work. I guess you can clean all right. But you can't cook."

"Yes, I can. Well, a few things. I'll learn others, if I need to."

"Are you sure it'll be safe? Living with a man like that?" Maggie shivered, just like she'd done when they'd told ghost stories at slumber parties.

Sidonie suppressed an answering shiver. Rafe McMasters should not induce shivers in anyone, except maybe a clone of Cathy What's-her-name. He certainly was not her type. Oh, if what the judge and Maggie said were true, he might have been at one time—she was as much a sucker for bad boys as any red-blooded American female. But a rancher in banker's clothing? No way.

"A man like what? He might have been a trouble-maker when he was younger, but he's changed. Now he's an upright, uptight solid citizen. And you know there is nothing stuffier than a reformed rogue."

"Rafe McMasters?" Maggie's face fell. "Say it isn't so."

"Can't. The man's a dull, stodgy businessman. And, as far as I could tell on our short acquaintance, he's happy about it, to boot."

After leaving her friend's house, Sidonie swung by the vet's to pick up Gypsy. Bathed and groomed, she still looked like a mutt. "Never mind. I love you, anyway."

The telephone was ringing off the wall when she and Gypsy got home, and no one was there to answer it. Rafe must be giving her plenty of time to clear out. Sidonie hesitated only a second before picking up the receiver. It might be some poor woman looking for a job, one that had already been filled.

Rafe McMasters might not know it yet, but he had a housekeeper. Her.

"Hello. McMasters residence."

"Hello. Who's this? Don't tell me—I might have known he wouldn't waste any time. Boy thinks he's wasted too much time already."

"Who is this?"

"Fielding. Cornelius Fielding. I thought he might have gotten tired of country life by now, be ready to come back to the Windy City. Plenty of women here, I told him. Plenty of other business opportunities, too, if he became bored with commodity trading. But he's had his mind made up, and nothing I offered could change it. Three things he wanted and now I guess he's got them all."

"Cornelius Fielding?" The man was talking a mile a minute, but his name had registered. "The billionaire?"

"Please. Multibillionaire. The richest man in the United States—except for that computer genius, darn him. Fat lot of good it does me, if I can't keep a good man on the payroll. What's your name, young lady? He must have swept you right off your feet. Fast worker, that Rafe McMasters. Always has been. Saved my life, you know. That's how we met. Been working for me ever since, until he finally got enough money to execute his plan. Rafe's big on planning things out, you know. First part was easy—knew he'd get that part. Land and a house. All that takes is money, and I did teach him a thing or two about making money. But I thought finding a woman, the right woman, would have been harder. It should have been. Especially one with all those essentials.''

"Essentials?" The man was talking so fast, Sidonie could barely keep up.

"Qualifications he said he wanted for his wife. Told him he shouldn't set his standards too high. Not too low, either. But perfection's hard to come by. No offense, but I thought maybe he'd never find you. What did you say your name was? See it on the wedding invitation, I know, but I like to know what to call the people I care about.''

"Sidonie. Sidonie Saddler. And I don't have any idea what you're talking about. Rafe works for you?"

"Worked. For almost fifteen years. Told me from the first he'd be moving on when he was ready to go after his dream. Not in those words, you understand. Rafe says he doesn't dream, he plans. Whatever he calls it, it looks like he's done it—gotten the whole kit and caboodle. The land, the house and the woman. You be good to him. Rafe McMasters deserves the best.''

"Mr. Fielding, you've—"

"Corny, call me Corny. I'm going to be godfather to your children. Didn't he tell you that? You don't object, do you? Good thing to have a multibillionaire as a godfather.''

"No kidding. But, Corny—"

"Sid—what did you say your name was again? Sidney?"

"Sidney with an *o* in the middle. Sid-oh-nee."

"Well, Sidonie, I like you. 'Fraid I wouldn't, you know. Rafe's idea of an ideal woman wasn't mine. So, when's the wedding?"

"I have no idea. I'm not his fiancée, I'm his housekeeper."

"Housekeeper?"

"Well, he doesn't know it yet, but I'm applying for the job. He's living in my house, and he advertised for a housekeeper. I want to stay here, and I don't mind cooking and cleaning, so it should work out. Don't you think?"

"My, my. This sounds interesting. How did he end up in your house?"

"He rented it. Behind my back."

"Not like Rafe to be underhanded—"

"Oh, he wasn't. My financial guardian rented the house to him while I was in New York, not knowing that I would need it. I've decided not to evict Mr. McMasters, as long as he lets me stay here with him." She paused. "You know him better than I do. What do you think? Will he go for it?"

"You don't sound like any housekeeper I ever met. How much experience do you have?"

"None. But how hard can it be to keep a house clean? I'm not afraid of work."

"Can you cook?"

"Sort of."

"What do you do, Sidonie? Interesting name, that. Don't think I've ever heard it before."

"My mother wanted an unusual name for me—one that would look good on a marquee."

"Ah. You're an actress."

"No. A dancer. But I hurt my knee and I need a place to stay while I get back in shape. I thought I had one, but then I got here—"

"A dancer? Who can't cook." Cornelius chuckled. "Tell me, young lady, what do you look like?"

"I'm tall, five feet eight inches, red hair, blue eyes. And Rafe doesn't think I'm a lady. Why?"

"Lady or not, you sound like the right woman to me—just the person to teach that boy what really is essential in a marriage."

"I don't want to marry him. I want to live with him. I mean, I just want to live in my house. As his housekeeper. Do you think he'll agree to that?"

"If Rafe doesn't hire you, or marry you, you come to Chicago and look me up. I've been a widower for twenty years—thought I'd never find another wife as good as the first one, but you might change my mind. And, Sidonie, tell him I said to remember my motto— Never Pass Up An Opportunity."

"I'm not sure he'll think of me as an opportunity."

"If he doesn't, he's a fool."

Chapter Three

"All right, Miss Saddler. You're hired."

She flashed him a smile that made his knees go as weak as his head. He had to be soft in the head—he'd just agreed to make Sidonie Saddler his housekeeper.

His live-in housekeeper. He'd have to move, of course. No way could he live under the same roof with her—not if he wanted a rat's chance in a maze of courting any of the ladies in the county. No decent woman would put up with a chorus girl, even if she were disguised as a housekeeper.

Rafe pushed himself away from the kitchen counter he'd been leaning on and headed for the door. "Come into the study and I'll give you your instructions." Wrestling with his problem—how to keep Sidonie safe and himself sober and respectable—made the words come out curt and cold. He was halfway down the hall before he realized she wasn't following him. He glanced over his shoulder.

Sidonie was standing in the doorway to the kitchen.

When he caught her eye, she said coolly, "I'll be with you as soon as I feed Gypsy."

He should have known Sidonie wasn't going to be a subservient kind of servant. "Gypsy? Oh, that's what you named the mutt. I guess she'll be staying, too."

"That's all right, isn't it?"

For the first time that afternoon, Sidonie looked worried. Mostly she'd been doing a great imitation of a steamroller. She'd flattened him out in a New York minute.

"Yeah, the dog can stay." Rafe made a disgusted noise as he stomped to his study. What had he done? A woman like her living in the same house was the last thing he needed. Housekeeper? Ha! No one was going to buy that story. Sidonie sure as hell didn't look like a woman who knew how to cook and clean.

But she was hurt, and her injury reminded him of his own knee problem years ago, the injury that had ended his career as a rodeo cowboy. He'd come to this very place to heal—first his body and later his heart. After he'd recovered, Buck Saddler had loaned him a stake, enough money for a new start in another place. Buck had been thrown from a horse and killed before Rafe could pay him back.

Rafe had decided that leasing Buck's ranch house for twice the going rate would finally wipe out the old liability. Apparently his way wasn't good enough for whatever fate had sent Buck's daughter home. Helping Sidonie was going to be the interest on the debt.

Rafe couldn't turn Sidonie away from her own home, not after all Buck Saddler had done for him, not when she was hurting and looking for a safe place to curl up and lick her wounds. She needed time to figure out what she was going to do with the rest of her life. He'd been there. He knew what it was like to have the future you'd planned blow up in your face.

Rafe sat down at his desk, put his face in his hands and groaned. He'd always had a weak spot for strays and underdogs, but he'd never adopted a chorus girl before. With her flaming red hair, blue eyes and long, long legs, Sidonie was bound to cause trouble. And trouble was something he'd sworn he was going to stay away from the day he left Cache. With one notable exception—the night he'd first met Cornelius Fielding—he'd kept his vow.

And he was his own man, now. No one was going to mistake him for someone who could be bought this time around.

He leaned back and stared at the door, squaring his jaw. No redheaded, blue-eyed temptress was going to lead him around like a bull with a ring through his nose. The fact that his unwanted houseguest had wakened his long-dormant hormones was just bad timing. A few more weeks and he'd be engaged, and his hormones could rage all they wanted to. He could wait.

The cause of his dilemma strolled through his study door, a satisfied smile on her face. He couldn't fault her for looking smug. He had met her less than twenty-four hours ago, and she'd gotten everything she'd wanted from him so far. That had to stop. If he didn't let her know right now who was the boss of this outfit, no telling what she'd be up to next.

''Sit.'' He nodded at the chair in front of his desk.

''Standing's more comfortable. My knee.'' She pointed to the brace on her left leg.

He cleared his throat and tried again. ''Your duties are—''

"Oh, I know. I cook your meals, clean the house...do your laundry. In a day or two I'll know whether you wear boxers or briefs." She winked at him, a slow, sexy wink, and his toes curled in his loafers.

He held up a hand. "Let me do this, all right? I'd like to feel like I'm the one in charge." She shot him a surprised look, but she kept her mouth shut for a change. "I expect breakfast on the table at six, lunch at noon and dinner at six. I want real food, meat and potatoes. No quiche, no pasta and no fancy French sauces. Understand?"

She nodded. That worried look flashed across her face again. Damn. She probably didn't even know how to cook something simple. On top of everything else, he was going to starve. He shifted his gaze away from Sidonie. He couldn't look at her—if she batted those baby blues at him one more time, he'd be agreeing to sweep and dust and bring her breakfast in bed.

Staring out the window, he continued. "I'll let you know if I'm not going to be here at mealtime. I'm stocking my ranch, so I'll be doing a lot of traveling in the next few months—visiting ranches with breeding stock, going to cattle auctions here and in the neighboring counties. We probably won't see that much of each other." He hoped.

When he forced himself to meet her gaze, he caught her grinning at him. She sobered immediately and nodded. "Is that all?"

"No. When I'm away, you'll be responsible for feeding and watering the stock on this place. Right now that's only my horse and one Beefmaster steer, but there's more on the way. The breeding stock I buy will have to stay here until my barn and corrals are finished. Can you handle it?''

"Sure.'' She frowned. "I've heard of Longhorns and Shorthorns, Angus and Herefords, but what's a Beefmaster?''

"Another breed of cattle. Tom Lasater developed it—breeding for six essential traits.''

Sidonie's big blue eyes got bigger. "Essentials? Where have I heard that—'' She grinned at him again. "Never mind. You were saying?''

"Beefmasters are bred for six essential traits— weight, conformation, milking ability, fertility, hardiness and disposition—traits that make for good commercial beef cattle.''

"Whatever.'' She half turned toward the door. "I'll get started on dinner.''

"Not yet. I'm not finished.'' He stood up. "This room is off-limits. Don't come in here without an invitation, and don't expect to be invited.'' Rafe needed a hideout, at least one place guaranteed to be a Sidonie-free zone, or he'd never survive the next three months.

Narrowing her eyes, she looked around the room. "Secrets?'' she asked in an exaggerated stage whisper.

She was laughing at him, plain as day. That should have made him angry. Instead he had to work at keeping a grin off his face. "Darn right. Deep, dark secrets. And they're going to stay that way. Understand?''

She shrugged and turned to go again.

"Wait! There's one more thing,'' he said. She stopped and pirouetted around to face him. "This is important, Sidonie.'' He took a breath and pinned her with a stern look. "Don't flirt with me.''

Her eyebrows shot up. "I beg your pardon?''

"I don't want anyone thinking we have anything but a business relationship. This is a small town, and people talk."

"So I've been told. And you don't want them talking about us."

"That's too much to hope for. I just don't want them thinking you and I..."

"Have the hots for each other?" She stuck her nose in the air. "Not a problem. I don't go for stuffed shirts."

Not a problem for her, maybe. But his shirt didn't feel stuffed to him—his chinos, however, were another story. "Good. And, Sidonie, when you're in town, or around other people, keep a low profile, will you? Try not to do anything outrageous."

"Outrageous? I'm not sure I know what you mean." She frowned and pursed her lips. "Unless...would posing for a centerfold qualify as outrageous?"

"Centerfold? You posed for *Playboy*?" Picturing Sidonie with a staple in her navel made his eyes glaze over.

"Don't be silly. What would a *Playboy* photographer be doing in Cache, Texas? Dr. Jones asked me to pose for the *Veterinarian Times*. He's the editor, and he said he wants to increase circulation."

"The vet asked you to pose nude?" Rafe shoved a hand through his hair, outraged. That dirty old codger!

"Not nude." She gave him a severe look. "Where is your mind, Mr. McMasters? In overalls. He did say something about leaving one strap unhooked—"

"You can't do it. No way." He could see one of her lush breasts falling out of a pair of overalls with no trouble at all. Rafe began to sweat. "Doc Jones said he wanted you to help him sell more magazines? You didn't fall for that line, did you?"

Sidonie let loose a whoop of laughter. "I didn't fall for anything, but you sure did. Lighten up, McMasters. I made the whole thing up. There is no centerfold in the *Veterinarian Times*, but, judging by your reaction, maybe there should be. I'll be sure and mention it to the doctor next time I take Gypsy in for her shots."

With a growl, Rafe grabbed his hat off the hat rack next to the desk. Jamming it on his head, he told her, "I'm going to feed and water the stock."

Feeling like he'd just gone ten rounds with George Foreman, Rafe didn't notice that Sidonie was limping along behind him until she yelled at him to slow down. He stopped and waited for her. "Shouldn't you be fixing supper?"

Panting a little, just enough to part her lips and make her mouth look more delicious than ever, she caught up with him. "I thought you wanted to show me how to take care of the horse and the cow."

"Steer."

"Right. Steer. And I forgot to give you a message. Corny called while you were out."

"Corny—you mean Cornelius Fielding?"

"Yes."

"What did he want? Did he say?"

"He wanted to know how your plan was coming along. Oh, and he said to tell you to remember his motto."

"Never Pass Up An Opportunity. What opportunity was he talking about?"

"Me, but I told him you wouldn't think of me as an opportunity—more of a dilemma." She grinned at him. "Now, what is it you want me to do?"

Rafe almost grabbed her. He'd show her exactly what he wanted her to do. Wrap herself around him, so close that he'd feel her every breath as if it were his. Kiss him on the mouth, slow and soft at first, then hard and fast with her mouth open and her tongue tangling with his.

Stifling a groan, he covered the remaining distance to the barn in record time, leaving Sidonie to follow as best she could. He'd almost recovered from his erotic fantasizing by the time Sidonie caught up with him. Tequila, his horse, was in a stall in the barn. The steer was in a corral with a lean-to attached so the animal could get out of the sun or rain when necessary. Careful not to touch her, Rafe showed Sidonie where the feed was, how much to give each animal and how to fill the water troughs.

Sidonie stroked Tequila's nose and scratched behind his ears, all the while crooning silly words to the stallion. Tequila looked very happy. And why not? Any male being stroked and petted by a sexy redhead would be ecstatic. Rafe had never been jealous of his horse before, but he was seriously considering having the stallion gelded before he realized what he was thinking.

With a shudder he grabbed Sidonie by the hand and led her outside to the corral where the Beefmaster was penned. She was almost over the fence before Rafe stopped her. "Where do you think you're going?"

"To make friends with the calf. You said he couldn't hurt me."

"He can't gore you. His horns haven't come in yet. But he outweighs you by a few hundred pounds. If you get too close he could cause serious damage."

Sidonie eyed the steer. "He doesn't look mean. I

don't believe he'd hurt me. Would you, baby?'' She started over the fence again.

Rafe grabbed her from behind, his hands around her waist. For one weak moment he almost gave in to the urge to haul her back against him, but he locked his elbows and kept her at arm's length. ''Stay out of the corral, Sidonie. That's an order.''

Sidonie wiggled out of his grasp and turned to face him. She saluted. ''Yes, sir! Anything you say, boss man.''

Narrowing his eyes, Rafe growled, ''Anything?'' He moved closer. A man could only stand so much. Maybe it was time to take a bite of the fruit he'd deliberately put in the ''forbidden'' category. One taste might be enough to get over this sudden craving for redheaded trouble. He reached for her.

Sidonie backed up a step, stumbled and fell on her shapely butt.

Rafe held out his hand, and when she'd grasped it, he pulled her to her feet. ''Damn! I keep forgetting you're hurt. Are you okay? I'm sorry I made you fall down.''

''It wasn't your fault. I'm clumsy with the brace on.'' Dusting off her backside, she asked, ''Well, what do I feed him?''

''Corn. It's in the barn.'' He showed her the storage bin filled with dried corn and measured out the correct amount. They returned to the corral, and poured the corn into the feed trough.

Sidonie rested her arms on the top rail of the corral fence and stared at the steer. ''He's beautiful. A redhead, just like me. Except he's more of a strawberry blond.'' She looked at Rafe with narrowed eyes. ''And you're going to—'' She stopped and spelled out the word. ''*C-o-o-k* him?''

''That's right. If you behave, I'll let you have one of his fillets.''

She turned around and clapped her hands over his mouth. ''Be quiet! He'll hear you.'' She hissed the words.

''He doesn't understand,'' Rafe muttered against Sidonie's soft palm. Her hand touching his mouth was making him have evil thoughts again. Maybe he should revert to type for a week or two—indulge in his trademark bad-boy behavior before he settled down—

He shoved her hands away. Sidonie was injured, damn it. Not fair game for his libido. Not to mention that he was taking care of her to repay his debt to her father.

''You can't be sure he doesn't know you're going to eat him.''

''Yes, I can. He's a dumb animal.''

''He's a noble beast. What's his name?''

''He doesn't have a name.''

''Well, I'll think of one. I did a pretty good job of naming the dog, didn't I?'' She started back toward the house.

''Sidonie, the dog is a pet. The steer is not. He's going to be dinner for the townspeople of Cache. You can't name something you're going to eat.''

''Cannibal,'' she accused.

''Oh, Lordy. You're not a vegetarian, are you?''

That stopped her in her tracks. Her mouth worked, but nothing came out. She had a guilty look about her eyes.

''Well, are you?''

"N-no." Her chin came up. Sidonie's flashes of weakness never lasted longer than the blink of an eye, it seemed. "But I'm considering it."

"Well, consider it after you cook supper. There are a couple of steaks in the refrigerator." He strode past her.

Sidonie trailed after him, a pensive look on her face. She hadn't thought about where meat came from for years. She had no trouble recalling the first time she made the connection.

Her father had given her an orphan lamb to feed. She'd given the little fellow bottle after bottle of warm milk, laughed at its antics and fallen in love. Then one morning when she'd gone to feed her pet, it had been gone. Her father had taken the lamb, her lamb, to auction. Buck had tried to give her the money he'd gotten for the lamb, but she'd knocked it out of his hand and cried her eyes out.

Years of buying meat shrink-wrapped in plastic had dulled the memory. She winced when she thought of all the lamb chops she'd eaten since then. She glanced over her shoulder. The Beefmaster was calmly munching the grain they'd given it. She wasn't going to have her heart broken over a great huge steer. A seven-hundred-pound Beefmaster was not a cute little lamb. She wouldn't get attached to it. She wouldn't.

But she was in danger of getting more attached than she should to the steer's owner. Her palm still tingled where his mouth had pressed against it. And those heated looks he'd sent her way... She'd been sure a time or two that he was going to kiss her. She was sorry he hadn't. Kissing Rafe McMasters might turn out to be the sensual experience of a lifetime. But he was fighting the attraction. Why? Corny had said he was looking for a woman.

But not just a woman, a wife. He sure wouldn't want to marry a dancer, that was obvious. That was okay. This chorus girl wasn't interested in settling down. All she wanted was her home.

Only until she could dance again, she reminded herself. She wasn't ready to retire to the country permanently. The problem was, Rafe was too darn appealing for her own good. A man trying so hard not to be bad was a tough challenge to resist. She'd have to do it, though. She'd avoided short-term relationships all her life—she'd never been in one place long enough for the other kind—and now was not the time to indulge herself. No matter how tempted she was.

Sidonie walked into the kitchen, went to the refrigerator and found the steaks. The neatly packaged red meat bore no resemblance to the steaks-on-the-hoof she'd left in the corral. Her mouth watered. She was hungry. And she knew how to broil a steak. Ruthlessly suppressing the memory of the steer's trusting brown eyes, Sidonie got out the broiler pan. She put two Idaho potatoes in the oven to bake and looked for salad makings.

When the meal was ready, she went to find Rafe. He was in his study, behind closed doors. She knocked once, then entered. "Supper's ready. Do you want to eat in the kitchen or the dining room?"

"Kitchen's okay."

"Does the hired help get to eat at the same table?"

"Yep."

He kept up his inadvertent Gary Cooper imitation all through dinner. Sidonie could talk a mile a minute, but she ran out of steam around the seventy-fourth

"Yep." Actually she'd heard more "nopes" than "yeps."

"Why did you come back to Proffit County?"

"No place like home."

His tone was sardonic, but his brown eyes were wistful. Not to mention warm and trusting. Not unlike the Beefmaster's. Once she'd been reminded of the steer, the bite of steak Sidonie had been chewing on suddenly tasted a lot like sawdust. She swallowed and tried conversation again.

"You still think of this part of Texas as your home? After being away for so long?"

He nodded. "I always planned to come back someday."

"Why?"

Rafe ignored her query. "You left Proffit County almost as many years ago as I did. You came back."

"But I don't intend to stay. Not this time. Maybe years from now when I'm too old to dance I'll come back here to retire. Or maybe I'll stay in New York. Or Los Angeles."

"I think you'll come back here. This is where your roots are."

"Roots? I don't need roots—I'm not a tree. I only came back to Cache this time because I needed a cheap place to stay. Free is as cheap as it gets."

"You've got roots, whether you want to admit it or not. You're Buck Saddler's daughter, pioneer stock. The Saddlers settled this part of Texas, along with the Clancys and the Longstreets and a few of my ancestors."

Sidonie opened her mouth to argue with him, but thought better of it. Now that he was talking in complete sentences, maybe she could get him to talk about his three-pronged plan—land, house, woman. For some reason Rafe's plan intrigued her, especially the "woman" part. Finding out what kind of woman Rafe was looking for was not terribly important, of course, but she couldn't help being curious.

"Judge Longstreet said you're building the biggest house in the county. Why do you need so much room? Are you going to have a large family?"

"Maybe."

"So I guess that would involve getting married. Got anyone in mind?"

"Maybe. Any more steak?"

"No." She shoved her plate across the table. "You can have the rest of mine. I've lost my taste for beef."

Rafe almost choked. "Never say that to a cattleman," he sputtered. Stabbing her leftover steak with his fork, he transferred it to his plate.

"You know everyone in town is talking about you?"

He swallowed and wiped his mouth with his napkin. His only response was a shrug of his broad shoulders. "That's small towns for you."

"You can't blame them. You're a mystery. Everyone wonders where you've been and why you came back to Cache."

Rafe's brown eyes narrowed shrewdly. "Everyone? Or just you?"

"Me? Why would I be curious about you? Anyway, I know where you've been. In Chicago, working for Cornelius Fielding."

"You're sure about that? Fielding Enterprises has businesses all over the world, including a few ranches here and there."

Sidonie looked at the button-down collar peeking

out of his crewneck sweater. "I don't think you've been ranching for the past fifteen years. You don't even own a pair of jeans, do you?"

"I may have an old pair packed away in a trunk."

"From your rodeo days?"

"People *have* been talking about me, haven't they? And you've been listening. Why so interested in me, Sidonie?"

"I'm not. Not particularly. Like you said—it's a small town. Nothing much to do. How did you hook up with Fielding?"

"That's nobody's business but mine."

Sidonie threw up her hands in disgust. "It's that attitude that's getting you talked about. Why keep your past a secret? If people knew where you've been for the past fifteen years, and what you've been doing, they would stop speculating about you." She didn't believe that for a minute, but it might make him reconsider keeping up his imitation of a clam.

She wanted to ask why he'd left Cache. And why he'd jilted Susie Q or whatever the paragon's name was, but instinct warned her not to push too hard. If Rafe balked at confirming the answers she already knew, he wasn't going to open up about personal matters. The man sure liked his privacy. Almost as much as she liked invading it.

"I bet someone ran you out of town fifteen years ago, and you've come back to settle that old score."

He shot her a surprised look. "Where'd you get a fool idea like that? You show business people sure have a flare for melodrama." Standing up, he carried his empty plate to the sink. "It's a safe bet people are talking about you, too, and why you came back to Proffit County."

"Why I came back isn't a secret. I needed a place to stay until my knee's better."

"You need more than a place to stay. You need someone to look after you, too. Don't you have a mother somewhere? That woman who left Buck? Why didn't you go to her to recuperate?"

"She's working. In England."

"She's not still dancing, is she? Good Lord. The woman must be pushing fifty."

"She's forty-eight, her name is Belle, and she's a choreographer." She stood up and began clearing the table. Rafe was beginning to annoy her. Every time she got close to finding out what she wanted to know, he said something that sent her off in another direction. She narrowed her eyes. It wasn't accidental. He was trying to divert her attention from his business to hers.

"Belle. That's right." Rafe took the dishes from her hands and stacked them in the sink.

"Well, of course it's right. I do know my own mother's name."

Leaning against the counter with his arms crossed over his chest, he said, "Too bad Buck had to fall for someone like her."

"Someone like—what does that mean?"

"A woman who leaves a man with an empty bed and a broken heart."

Her hands on her hips, Sidonie glared at him. "What was between my father and my mother is none of *your* business. But just to set you straight—Belle loved my father right up until the day he died. She was the best thing that ever happened to him."

"I'm not sure Buck would agree with that."

"Did you ever hear him say anything against my mother?"

"No, but he wouldn't. Buck was a gentleman."

"And Belle's no lady, is that it?"

"Your words, not mine." He had a self-satisfied smirk on his face. He thought he'd gotten her side-tracked for good, now.

Sidonie took a deep breath, then let it out slowly through slightly parted lips. No self-righteous prig was going to insult her mother and get away with it. She'd teach Rafe McMasters a thing or two about women. She knew just how to do it.

Sidonie let the tip of her pink tongue glide slowly over her top lip. Sure enough, Rafe's grin got a tad lopsided as his gaze shifted from her eyes to her mouth. Satisfied that her plan would work, Sidonie moved closer, trapping him against the counter. "Lady or not, I still say my mother was the best thing that ever happened to Daddy."

"What are you up to, Sidonie?" Now he looked downright nervous.

Sidonie stood on tiptoe and whispered huskily into his ear, "I'm a lot like my mother, Rafe. I could be the best thing that ever happened to you." She skimmed her hands up the front of Rafe's sweater, barely touching him.

The slight contact was enough to make his muscles tense and his breathing ragged. He grabbed her hands. Sensing Rafe was trying—weakly—to push her away, Sidonie leaned into him, molding her body to his. With a groan he released her hands and wound his arms around her waist. He lowered his head to hers.

Sidonie swallowed a triumphant grin the moment before his lips touched hers. Now was the time to pull back and let him fall flat on his handsome face. But she hesitated a second too long, and their mouths joined. Once his lips touched hers she was lost.

She'd never felt such pleasure from a kiss. She was drowning in pleasure, going under once, twice, three times. Sidonie responded with enthusiastic ardor, clinging like a honeysuckle vine to Rafe's shoulders. She whimpered with frustration when the plastic brace kept her from climbing his body and wrapping her legs around his waist.

Rafe shifted one hand to her bottom and urged her closer, all the while keeping his lips molded to hers, sending his tongue on sensuous forays into her mouth.

Then it was over.

He took his mouth from hers and pushed her away. "Damn! Damn! Damn!"

He shoved his hands in his hair, making it stand up in adorable spikes. Sidonie reached up to smooth his hair, and he batted her hand away.

"Damn it all to hell!"

Feeling ridiculously hurt by his reaction to a kiss that had left her breathless, Sidonie managed to say, with almost believable nonchalance, "Are you upset about something?"

"Upset? Why would I be upset? I just attacked you—you, someone I'm supposed to look after—and this is only your first day on the job!"

He really was losing it. For some reason that went a long way toward reviving her sagging spirits.

"You didn't attack me—it was the other way around. It wasn't your fault," she said, willing to be magnanimous under the circumstances.

Then the other thing he'd said registered. "'Take care of me'? What does that mean?" she blustered.

"Never mind, I know exactly what it means. You think I'm some kind of helpless female who needs a big, strong man to look after me."

His guilty look confirmed her suspicions. That explained a lot—like why he'd hired her to be his housekeeper after only token resistance. "You dumb so-and-so! I don't need looking after. I've been taking care of myself for years and years. I don't need a thing from you—"

She stopped.

But her job. She needed the job so she could stay in her house, on her ranch. Gritting her teeth, she told him as much. "If I had anyplace to go, I'd leave. But I don't. So I'm staying right here, whether you like it or not. But if you kiss me again, I'll tell the whole town how Rafe McMasters tried to seduce me."

He'd been staring at her with a clenched jaw, but that got his mouth working. "You'll what? No way. You started it. Shoving me up against the counter—"

She threw up her hands. "All right, all right! I take that back. I won't start any gossip. But don't think I *wanted* to kiss you—I was only trying to teach you a lesson."

"What lesson?"

"Why Buck might have been happy with Belle, even if they didn't see much of each other after she went back to work."

"I don't know what you're talking about. He didn't see her at all after she left town."

"Oh, yes, he did. They'd meet two or three times a year. Whenever she was in a road show that got close enough to Cache for him to come see her, or whenever he felt like a trip to New York."

His mouth dropped open, then snapped shut.

"Dad never told you about his trips?"

"No."

"He was probably embarrassed. He didn't like people talking about him and Mom. Any more than you'd like people talking about you and—" She stopped abruptly.

"See? I'm not the only one concerned with privacy. And propriety. Your own father—"

"Oh, shut up. I get the picture. And the point." Taking a deep breath, she managed to rein in her temper. "I'll be a good little employee from now on, I promise. And I'll see to it that no one has any reason to talk about us."

He eyed her warily. "What have you got in mind?"

"Nothing yet. I'll figure out something."

"Do that. I'm going to my study."

Sidonie leaned against the kitchen counter and touched her fingers to her mouth. It wasn't fair. Her lips were still tingling, but Rafe hadn't had any trouble walking away from her. Or maybe he had. Maybe he'd been *running* away, afraid he wouldn't be able to resist kissing her again if he stayed in the same room with her.

She liked that reason for his hasty departure. But she couldn't be sure he'd left because he'd feared being overwhelmed by passion. Sidonie pushed away from the counter and started after Rafe. She'd never know until she asked. Before she caught up with him, the study door closed with a bang.

She started to knock, then remembered what he'd said. The study was off-limits to her. Sidonie eyed the closed door speculatively.

What was he hiding in there?

Chapter Four

At five o'clock the next morning, Sidonie slapped the alarm button on the clock without opening her eyes. Her brain woke up, anyway, and its traitorous first thought was that Rafe McMasters was a great kisser. Maybe even an Olympic-class kisser. She'd have known for sure, if the kiss had lasted a few seconds longer. But it hadn't, and Rafe didn't seem inclined to go for the gold.

Inclined, ha! The last thing Rafe wanted was to kiss her again. He might be attracted to her, but he'd made it clear he didn't want to be. He'd stayed locked in his study until after she'd gone to bed.

She tossed back the covers and sat up. She didn't care. Rafe was wrong about almost everything, except that the two of them weren't right for each other. For all kinds of reasons, starting with her being a city girl and him being a country boy. That was the difference that had doomed her parents' marriage to little more than an erratic affair.

Too bad, she thought, yawning and stretching. She had discovered that underneath that stuffed shirt beat the heart of a nice man, an honorable man. Not to mention a sexy man who was a great kisser.

She was tempted to save him from himself.

A cold nose shoved into her hand brought Sidonie out of her reverie. "Nah! I'm not looking for romance on the range. Or sex in the sagebrush. I don't have time to teach him how much fun I can be. He'll just have to stay a fuddy-duddy." She scratched Gypsy behind the ears. "Now that we've gotten that little kiss behind us, we'll get along just fine. He can buy his cows and practice being a sanctimonious prig worthy of his ideal woman, and I can work on getting back in shape."

The dog pricked up her floppy ears and cocked her head to one side.

Swinging her legs to the floor, Sidonie gingerly tested her knee before putting her full weight on it. It seemed to be working all right. She stood up and stretched luxuriously. Gypsy barked sharply.

"You don't think we'll get along? Well, after ten years of working with a bunch of prima donnas in tutus, I can get along with anyone. I could tell you stories..." Yawning, she stretched again.

"And it really is better that Rafe and I don't get along too well. The chemistry is there, but this is not the time to set up a lab and experiment. That could lead to all kinds of complications. Like I said before, I don't have time for a man right now. And if I did, it wouldn't be Rafe McMasters. He's too— And he doesn't— Not only that, I prefer—" She threw up her hands. "What I'm trying to say is when—if—I do decide to settle down, it won't be with someone who thinks dancers are...bad girls. The bottom line is, right now I have more important things to do.''

Like walk the dog and exercise her knee. But duty first—her job description meant she had to have breakfast on the table for the cowardly cowboy by six o'clock. She had hired on as a housekeeper, even if it had been only a ploy to stay where she needed to be, and she was going to keep her end of the bargain.

Sidonie dressed quickly in pale pink tights and a matching leotard. She pulled on an oversize emerald green sweater, strapped on her brace and headed for the kitchen.

The only breakfast foods she found in the kitchen were bacon and eggs. ''Ugh! I can feel my arteries clogging. Remind me to put cereal on the grocery list, Gypsy,'' she muttered, looking through the cabinets until she found a cast-iron skillet. ''No reason for him to worry about cholesterol, I suppose,'' she said, turning on the gas burner and laying strips of bacon in the skillet.

''The truth is, the man doesn't have an ounce of fat on him.'' She could attest to that, having been in his arms on two occasions now. Rafe McMasters was all hard bone overlaid with muscle, with skin like warm leather—

''Ouch!'' Bacon grease splattered, burning her hand. She turned on the faucet and ran cold water over her injury. ''It was only a kiss. Stop thinking about it!'' she told herself sternly.

She forced herself to concentrate on cooking. She made a pot of coffee. When that was done, she fished the bacon out of the hot grease and put it on a platter. It wasn't *too* crisp, she decided, critically eyeing the charred strips. She turned back to the stove, leaving the bacon to congeal in the grease she'd transferred to the cold platter along with it, and started frying eggs. She tried for sunny-side up, but the yolks kept breaking, and the eggs ended up more scrambled than fried.

As she transferred the mess to the platter with the bacon, Rafe entered the kitchen. He was wearing an expensive suit, with a crisp white shirt and conservative tie.

"Is breakfast ready?"

"Yes." She pointed to the platter. "Help yourself. I don't eat that kind of thing."

Rafe poked at the eggs. "I'm not sure I do, either. What is it?"

"Fried eggs and bacon."

After what sounded like a muttered oath—but it could have been a prayer—Rafe took a tentative bite. Then he got up and carried the platter to the counter. Dumping the contents into the sink, he turned on the disposal. In a gravelly voice that matched the disposal's irritating grind, he said, "Start over."

Sidonie opened her mouth to argue, but guilt had her holding her tongue and reaching for the skillet. The greasy mess she'd put in front of him hadn't been her best effort. She had overcooked the eggs and burned the bacon. But it wasn't entirely her fault breakfast had been ruined. She couldn't be blamed for the state of the pantry. "How about some oatmeal? That's better for you than all that fat. I could run to the store—"

Brown eyes turned steely. "Bacon. Crisp, but not charred. Eggs. Three. Over easy, if you think you can manage it. Scrambled, if not. Biscuits are probably not in the cards, so toast will do. Coffee—"

"I made coffee!"

"Make it again, and this time use a filter. I've got coffee grounds between my teeth from your first effort."

"Filter?" she asked blankly.

"They're in the pantry, right next to the coffee. You put one in the basket before you add the coffee. And while you're at it, make it stronger. This stuff tasted like dishwater." He stood up and walked to the back door. Putting on a camel hair topcoat, he took a fedora off the hat rack. Sidonie sneered. Some rancher he was. The man didn't even own a Stetson or a pair of boots. Today he was wearing a three-piece suit, white shirt and wing tips.

"Call me when it's ready. I'm going to feed and water the stock."

"Dressed like that? I thought that was my job."

"Only when I'm not around." He put on his hat, pulling the brim down so she couldn't see his eyes. "Which will be most of the time, after today."

He left, closing the door behind him.

"Well, tall, dark and grouchy, I won't miss you when you're gone." Punctuating her words with banging pots, and slamming cabinet doors, Sidonie stormed around the kitchen. "Filters! What does he think I am, Gypsy, stupid? I knew about filters. I just forgot. Geez, I'm a dancer, not a cook. He knew that when he hired me, so—"

Sidonie stopped her tirade. So why had he hired her? Pity? She could live with that. But apparently his compassion stopped short of eating badly cooked food. After a few minutes she had to admit she owed him better than she'd given so far.

"One country breakfast, coming up." She recooked bacon and eggs, carefully, and made a stronger pot of coffee—with a filter—then went to the back door and banged on the triangle hanging from the roof of the porch.

She waited until Rafe appeared at the barn door and signaled that he'd heard her, then went back inside. In a few minutes he entered the kitchen and sat down at the table. Sidonie put a plate in front of him.

"Bacon, crisp. Three eggs, scrambled. Toast, buttered, and coffee, filtered. Will this do?"

Nodding, Rafe shook out the napkin and laid it across his thighs. He ate silently. Chiding herself for the nervous knot in her stomach, Sidonie nibbled toast and sipped coffee. After a few minutes with no food going down the disposal, she finally relaxed enough to find some satisfaction in watching him eat what she had cooked for him. He wasn't complaining, and he was eating every bite.

This housekeeper gig might work out, after all.

After his last bite, Rafe leaned back in his chair and looked at her. She thought he was going to finally say something, maybe even something complimentary, but his gaze shifted from her eyes to her mouth. His stare, intense and seductive, made her lips tingle. He was remembering the kiss, she was sure of it. She was about to ask if he wanted to repeat the experiment, when he shifted his gaze again and caught her catching him ogling her mouth. Dark red patches appeared on his cheekbones. The shock of seeing a grown man blush made her swallow the flippant question she'd been about to ask.

He shoved away from the table. "I'll be in my study."

"Was breakfast all right?"

"Tolerable."

Deciding "tolerable" was good enough for a first—
well, second—effort, Sidonie cleaned the kitchen, then
went to her room. She gathered up a small tape player,
several exercise tapes, a towel and her ballet slippers
and put them in a canvas carryall. Shrugging into her
coat, she returned to the kitchen and went outside. She
crossed the backyard to a small outbuilding in a grove
of cottonwood trees.

She opened the door and screamed.

Rafe came running from the house. "Sidonie,
what's wrong? Did you hurt yourself?"

She glared at him. "Mr. McMasters. Are you responsible for this...desecration?" Sidonie pointed in
the open door.

Rafe moved closer and peered inside. "Hay? That's
what made you scream? Bales of hay?"

"It's not *what* they are. It's *where* they are. In my
studio!"

Stepping back from the door, Rafe let his gaze slide
over the wooden structure. "Is that what this building
is? I thought it was a chicken coop."

Sidonie tossed her head. It had been a chicken coop
at one time, but he didn't have to sneer at it. "It may
look like that on the outside, but you must have seen
the hardwood floors and the mirrored walls and the
barre when you were tossing hay in there."

"I might have, if I were the one who put the hay
there."

"You didn't do this?" she challenged, not ready to
let go of her righteous indignation.

"No, I didn't."

"Oh. I assumed..." She took a deep breath and
managed a conciliatory smile. If Rafe wasn't to blame,

she shouldn't take her disappointment out on him. Especially not if she wanted his help.

"The guys who delivered it put it there. I told them to, because there wasn't room in Buck's little barn. And my barn's not ready yet."

Sidonie gasped indignantly. "Well, you'll have to get it out."

"Why? You planning on raising a few chickens?"

She dropped the carryall and planted her fists on her hips. Glowering at him, she said, "No, I am not raising chickens. I need a place to do my exercises."

"I need a place to store hay. My lease covers the house and all outbuildings. Including the chicken coop."

"The chicken—studio is perfect for me. That's why I wanted to be here, so I'd be able to use it. Buck built it for me to use when I spent summers with him. It's my special place. I don't care what the damn lease says!" She stomped back to the studio and began tugging on the bale nearest the door. "If you won't move this hay, I will!"

Rafe walked up behind her, picked her up by the waist and pulled her away from the hay bale. "Don't be crazy. You can't move those bales by yourself. They weigh eighty or ninety pounds apiece."

"Well, help me. Or have your hands move them. Have you hired hands yet?"

"A couple. They're busy."

"Doing what? I thought you didn't have any cattle yet, except for Baby."

"Who's Baby?"

"The steer. You don't need cowboys for him, so what are your men doing?"

"They're building fences and corrals and such.

Why did you name him Baby? For that matter, why did you name him at all?''

"Well, he is a baby Beefmaster. You said he's only a year old. And I named him because...he needed a name.''

He gave her a dubious look. "I don't think so. But if it makes you happy..."

"Having the hay moved out of my studio will make me happy."

"I told you, there's no place to move the hay to. Won't be for another month or so. As soon as the barn on my place is ready, I'll have my men move the hay there.''

"A month?"

"At least."

"What about my exercises?"

"Use the parlor."

"I'll have to roll up the rug."

"Fine. Now that we've got that settled, I'm going to town. Tomorrow is auction day, and I'm meeting my foreman at the stockyards this morning to check out what's for sale." He picked up her carryall and started back to the house. "Coming?"

"Yes. I have to go to town today, too. I've got an appointment with Rayburn—Dr. Parker. At eleven-thirty. I may not be back in time to fix your lunch."

He had the gall to look relieved. "No problem. I'll grab a bite at the Pecan Café."

"Am I supposed to be cooking for your hands, too?"

"No. I've only hired a foreman and one other man, and they're both married. Their wives cook for them. Before I hired you, they were cooking for me, too."

"Where do they live?"

"On my place. The land I bought had a couple of houses on it—the old Johnson place, and that rock house down by Cowhouse Creek. They live there."

"Nice fringe benefit."

Rafe shrugged. "No sense in tearing down two perfectly good houses, when—"

"Wait a darn minute. You had two houses, and you had to lease mine? That doesn't make any sense."

"It does to me. Those houses were for my men. Besides, the other houses weren't close enough to where I'm building. I wanted to see my house going up." He opened the back door and let her precede him into the house. "Why are you seeing the doctor?"

"He just got my medical records, and he wants to examine my knee and go over my rehabilitation plan with me."

As they took off their coats and hung them on the rack, Rafe asked, "Shouldn't you be in a rehab hospital?"

"I was. For weeks and weeks. I broke out."

"You should have completed the treatment. The more exercise the better."

"Excuse me? I didn't know you'd gone to medical school, Dr. McMasters."

He ignored her sarcasm. "Maybe treatment has changed, but in my day the doctors said the more you exercise the knee, the more complete the recovery. Not that you'll ever be a hundred percent—"

"Whoa, there." Surprised by his familiarity with her kind of injury, she put a hand on his arm, stopping him. "It's your turn to back up. How do you know so much?"

"I banged up my knee pretty bad a few years back—when I was rodeoing."

"Which one? You don't limp. What was your treatment? Who was your doctor?"

"Right knee. And I do limp when I get tired. The treatment was as much exercise as I could stand, then fifteen minutes more."

"That hasn't changed. I didn't check myself out of the rehab center because they were working me too hard. They weren't pushing me enough. I'm used to four-hour dance classes at least once a day, and they were only working me for one or two hours at a time. I left because I needed more work, not less."

"You don't think you'll be able to dance again, do you?"

"I have to dance. That's all I know. You went back to the rodeo, didn't you?"

"No."

"But you kept on roping and riding in your day job, didn't you? Until you went to Chicago?"

"No."

Sidonie slanted a sideways look at Rafe. By the stubborn set of his jaw, she could tell he was not going to elaborate.

Rafe pulled out a chair and gently pushed her into it. "Any more coffee?"

"Yes, I made a fresh pot. And I remembered the filter this time, too."

He got two mugs from the cabinet and filled them. "Cream and two sugars, right?"

Sidonie nodded.

"What if you can't dance? Have you given any thought to what you'll do?"

"No. I will dance."

"Why is it so important to you? Can't be fame or fortune. You're only a—"

"A chorus girl? Don't be such a snob, McMasters. For most dancers, the chorus *is* fame and fortune. I've worked steadily for over ten years, on Broadway, off Broadway, off-off Broadway. I've been around the world twice, and I've played all the major, and quite a few minor, cities in the United States. Dancing is my life. I love everything about it from audition to closing night. Being a chorus girl gives me all I need—an opportunity to dance, to travel, to meet new people and see new things. Plus enough money for the basics—food, clothes...and a whole lot of fun."

He choked on his coffee. "Fun?"

"Haven't you heard? Chorus girls just want to have fun."

"I've heard. That's how Buck explained Belle's desertion. Country life wasn't 'fun' enough for her."

"Desertion? That's a little harsh, isn't it?" Sidonie asked in a deceptively mild tone. She wanted to dump the pot of boiling-hot coffee in his lap, but she restrained herself. She ought to be grateful Rafe was showing her his judgmental side. It made him much less appealing.

He put his coffee cup down and stood up. "Sorry. What happened between your parents is none of my business."

"Right," she muttered, gritting her teeth. Why did he have to apologize? And why did he have to look sheepish and sincere—a combination guaranteed to melt any woman's heart? Except hers. She was much too worldly and sophisticated to fall for an act like that. And it had to be an act. Rafe McMasters was not an "Aw, shucks" kind of guy.

Glancing at the kitchen clock, Rafe said, "I've got

to be going. I'll see you later. I will be home in time for supper."

"Okay. I'll be leaving in a few minutes, myself. Maybe I'll see you around town."

Rafe paled. He turned on his heel and walked out of the house without another word.

"Maybe not." Sidonie had the feeling he would cross the street if they happened to meet up strolling around the square. He must think that if the eligible women of Cache knew she and Rafe were—horrors!—living under the same roof, they'd shun him like the plague. She could tell him a thing or two. No woman was going to run away from man who looked like he looked and owned what he owned.

But then, any woman who'd be influenced by things like looks and money was shallow and mercenary—qualities that couldn't be what Rafe was looking for.

"What is important to him, Gypsy?"

The little dog cocked her head and followed Sidonie as she strolled down the hall. The study door was closed.

She tried the doorknob. "It's not locked. I think we'd better check it out, Gyp. He may have forgotten to close the window, too. We wouldn't want a burglar to get in and discover his secrets, would we?" She pushed the door open and entered the room.

Except for the brass lamp and a blank notepad, the desktop was bare. Sidonie sat down at the desk and opened a drawer. Gypsy growled.

"I'm only making sure nothing has been stolen." She opened another drawer. "Hmm. What have we here?" She pulled a leather-bound ledger out of the drawer and placed it on the desk.

The first few pages contained columns marked Assets and Liabilities. Sidonie's eyes widened at the number of zeros on the asset side. "Wow. He really is rich, Gypsy. But we already knew that."

She turned the pages until she reached one headed Essentials. "Aha! That word again." She scanned the page, reading aloud. "Calving ease. Weaning weight. Oh, pooh. It's more stuff about cows." Disgusted, she flipped another page. This one was also headed Essentials.

After scanning the page, Sidonie murmured, "Pay dirt." She reread the list out loud. "Respectable." Sidonie giggled. "No surprise there," she told Gypsy. She read on. "Country born and bred. Homemaker. Maternal. Attractive. Docile." She slammed the book shut. "Good grief! That's the kind of woman he wants? *Docile?* I don't believe it! If that's his idea of perfection, he's even stuffier than I thought. And he's choosing a wife the same way he's choosing a breed of cattle!"

Sidonie carefully replaced the ledger in the drawer and left the study. On the way to town she couldn't stop thinking about Rafe's search for the ideal rancher's wife. She decided he'd set himself an impossible goal. No real, live woman could have all the essential qualities he'd listed. Sidonie grinned. For some reason that made her feel better than she had all morning.

Her good mood lasted until the doctor's appointment. After that, things went downhill.

Rafe was smiling as he entered the house after returning from the cattle auction. He'd gotten a good deal on a small herd of crossbred cows. A few more cows, then an adequate number of range bulls, and his ranch would be up and running. Gypsy woofed a greeting, then returned to her vigil at the front window. The dog had been waiting there when he'd arrived home from the stockyards.

"Don't worry, dog. She'll be back. You can count on that."

He went to the front window and stared down the road for several minutes before he realized what he was doing. "Damn! I'm as bad as you are, Gypsy." The dog was already nuts about her new owner. Not surprising, since Sidonie had given the stray what all strays wanted—food, a place to stay and plenty of petting.

Come to think of it, that was what he wanted, too. He was aiming for more conservative packaging, but otherwise his desires weren't too different from Gypsy's. Grinning at his insight, Rafe reached down and scratched the little dog behind her ears. "How about that, Gypsy? We have something in common."

He straightened up and looked out the window again. Still no Sidonie. What was taking her so long? And why was he waiting for her like a besotted puppy? Disgruntled, he retreated to his study. Sidonie wasn't treating him like a stray. She'd tried to kick him out of his home, and she sure hadn't tried to charm him with food. Supper the night before hadn't been bad, although he preferred his steak rare, not cooked to death. But this morning! If he hadn't dumped her sorry excuse for breakfast down the disposal and made her start over, he'd have starved.

He sat down at his desk. And that outfit she'd sashayed around the kitchen in! Pink tights that showcased her spectacular legs and a sweater that left just enough to the imagination. Didn't the woman own any normal clothes?

He never should have hired her. There were other ways he could have paid Buck back. He could have written out a check for the amount he'd borrowed, plus a healthy dose of interest, and given it to her. Rafe reached for his checkbook. He could still do that, pay off his debt and give Sidonie her walking papers.

He wrote out the check, signing it with a flourish just as the front door opened and closed.

Sidonie was back. He tore the check from the book and went to meet her. The sooner he got this over with, the better. He'd tell her she could use her studio, of course, once they cleared out the hay. But she'd have to find another place to stay.

Pausing at the door to the parlor, he looked at her. She was slumped on the sofa, her head back, her eyes closed. Her injured leg was stretched out in front of her, and she was rubbing her left knee. Gypsy was standing in front of her, whining softly.

"What did Dr. Parker say?"

She opened her eyes a slit. "He thinks I'll lose the limp eventually."

"What about dancing?"

Her eyes opened wide, and he bit back an oath as he saw the pain there.

"He doesn't know what he's talking about. He doesn't know dancing, and he doesn't know me."

Rafe shoved the check in his pocket and sat down next to her, putting his arm around her shoulders. "What did he tell you?"

She sat up straighter, moving away from his touch. "How could Maggie have married a man like that? He's a quack."

"He told you chances are you'll never work as a dancer again, right?"

"Chances? He wasn't that encouraging. Dr. Parker said flat out that I could hang up my tap shoes. He said I'd never dance professionally again—the knee won't take that kind of punishment. Oh, I can fox-trot or tango all I want to. He even said I could teach. As if that's a life."

He pulled her back against his chest. She stiffened at first and tried to pull away, but he wouldn't let go. He hugged her closer. "Cry if you want to."

"I don't cry. Not ever." But she turned in his arms and put her head on his shoulder. "The doctor is wrong. He's a small-town family practitioner. He doesn't know about knee injuries."

"What did the orthopedic man say?"

After a few seconds, Sidonie sighed, her breath feathering against his neck. "The same thing. He was wrong and Rayburn's wrong! I will dance again. I *have* to dance again. I want my life back the way it was before—" She choked back a sob.

Rafe cuddled her closer. "Do you want to talk about it? What happened?"

"A stupid accident. I fell off the stage into the orchestra pit. Landed on my knee." She pulled away from him. "If I can't dance, maybe I have a future in slapstick comedy. Pratfalls a specialty. What do you think?"

"I think you'll find something you like just as much as dancing. Pratfalls could work."

"Well, I'm not changing careers just yet. I don't care what the doctors say. Doctors don't know everything."

"They don't know how stubborn you are, that's for sure."

"You make that sound like a fault."

"Isn't it?"

"Change *stubborn* to *persistent* and you have a virtue."

"That's true." He thought about the check crumpled in his pocket. He couldn't do it. Not after what she'd been through with the doctor. He owed Buck more than money, after all. Buck was the one who'd told him he'd done the right thing, walking away from Cathy Sue, when everyone else in town had condemned him. He owed Sidonie his support. And if the doctors were right, he'd help her find a new way to make a living.

He could start now.

"So the doc said you could fox-trot, hmm? And tango. Did you ever think about opening up a dancing school?"

"No."

"Maybe you should."

"Maybe you should mind your own business."

"I am. I need lessons."

"Oh, yeah? And just what do you think I could teach you, cowboy?"

"How to dance."

"You're serious."

"Yep."

"You really don't know how to dance?"

"Nope. And I need to learn before the Spring Dance at the country club."

"Wow! How can you be—what? Thirty-eight? Forty? And you never learned how to dance? Why not?"

"Thirty-five, and I just never learned, that's all."

"Not even the Texas two-step? I thought all cowboys knew that one."

"Not me." What in the hell was he doing? Having Sidonie in his arms was torture, and he was asking for more of the same? He let go of her. "Look, it was a bad idea. I don't need lessons."

"Oh, yes, you do." She threw her arms around his neck. "Everyone should know how to dance. Dancing is wonderful. I'll teach you."

"When do we start?"

"Now. Help me roll up the rug and move the furniture." She rummaged around in the carryall she'd left in the hall that morning, found the tape she was looking for and popped it in the player. "We'll start with the waltz."

"Waltz? Aren't there newer dances I should learn?"

"Later. First we waltz." She turned on the tape player. "Put your arm around my waist. Now, listen to the music—one-two-three, one-two-three—do you feel the rhythm?"

He felt the rhythm all right. And a whole lot more.

Chapter Five

A week later Rafe stood in the doorway of the parlor, watching Sidonie go through her exercise program. As usual, she was wearing only a leotard and tights. No bra. No panties. When he'd called her on it, she'd calmly explained that no ballet master allowed underwear—it ruined the lines of the body. Today she was barely covered in skintight silvery stuff that left nothing to the imagination. He imagined, anyway, feeling like a voyeur.

She moved gracefully from one impossible position to another, her concentration completely focused on her exercises. No doubt about it, he had to get her out of the house and away from him before he did something they'd both regret.

That scantily clad body and those supple moves had been giving him fits for days. He never should have suggested that she use the parlor for her workouts. Whenever he heard the music, he couldn't stay away. If she was in her studio, out of hearing, he wouldn't be tempted to drop everything and watch. He sure hoped his out-of-sight, out-of-mind plan would work. He had better things to do than imitate a Peeping Tom.

Look at her. She was bent over at the hip, touching her forehead to her knees, her cute little rear end pointed skyward. Rafe couldn't stifle a groan.

Sidonie slid her thighs apart, and looked up at him from between her legs. "Oh, hi. Are you ready for your lesson?" She straightened up and turned around.

"Yeah." As ready as he'd ever be. The lessons were sheer torture, masochistic exercises in self-restraint in the face of almost overwhelming temptation. What had he been thinking of when he'd asked her to teach him to dance?

Sidonie changed the CD on the player and moved toward him. He had to stiffen his whole body to keep from backing away from her.

"Okay, today we'll try something new. The cha-cha. Somewhat out-of-date, but people do occasionally try a Latin rhythm. Watch me."

She held one hand over her stomach and the other palm out at shoulder level. "Listen to the beat. One-two. One-two-three." She began to sway her hips seductively, moving her feet in quick, little steps.

Rafe walked to the stereo and turned it off. "No way. I'm not wiggling my butt for anyone."

She stopped dancing. Her hands went to her hips, and she tapped one foot on the floor. "You really are a stuffed shirt. No sense of adventure." She reached out and patted him on the rear. "And such a waste of cute buns, too."

He jumped. "No one in Cache, Texas, dances the cha-cha."

"You're probably right." She replaced the Latin

rhythms CD with another, and the familiar strains of "That Old Black Magic" filled the air. "All right, back to the basics. Shall we dance?"

She moved into his arms. He'd learned a lot the past week—that Sidonie's head just reached his chin, so that the wildflower scent of her hair filled his nostrils. That her cheek felt smooth and warm nestled in the hollow formed by his neck and shoulder. He closed his arms around her, and they began moving to the music. If he'd known how obligingly she would mold her body to his, how right she would feel in his arms, he never would have—

He muttered a curse. What *had* he been thinking of?

Oh, yeah. He'd wanted her to at least consider opening a dance studio. She was not cooperating. Sidonie continued to believe she could resume her career onstage and on the road. Some days she almost had him believing it. If hard work and determination were all it took, she'd have it made. But even Sidonie couldn't make a weak joint strong again.

She'd go for hours with no problem. But then the knee would give out. And not always at the end of one of her killer exercise sessions, when she was tired. It wasn't that predictable.

Not only that, spending what little spare time he had on dance lessons wasn't doing his plans much good, either. What with buying stock for his ranch and furniture for his new house, he still hadn't met any eligible women. Elise Prescott, the interior decorator he'd hired, had been broadcasting not-so-subtle messages that she was interested in more than his choice of window treatments, but she was a city girl. If he were going to change that essential requirement, he didn't have to go to Dallas to find an eligible candidate. He had a city girl right under his nose, in his arms.

He pulled her closer. He couldn't deny he was attracted to Sidonie. He'd have to be dead not to find her appealing. But she was not the woman for him, not by a long shot. Sidonie was not eligible for a lot of reasons. She was about as far from a rancher's wife as a woman could be. To begin with, Sidonie made it very clear that she couldn't wait to shake the dust of Proffit County off her dance shoes. She missed the bright lights of Broadway, the hustle and bustle of a big city. Her cooking had gotten a little better, he'd give her that, but it was still almost as unpredictable as her knee. Only last night she'd scorched the potatoes, and the gravy had been lumpy.

Those weren't her only faults, either. She was too softhearted for the reality of ranch life. She'd made a pet of every animal she'd gotten close to, including the main item on the menu for his housewarming party. Baby, the Beefmaster steer he'd been fattening up for the barbecue, followed Sidonie around like a puppy—a very large puppy.

Because of Sidonie, he'd had to order a side of beef from the meat locker. It was that or change the menu for his housewarming party from beef to chicken. Rafe twisted his mouth in disgust. What kind of cattle rancher served chicken at a barbecue?

He should back off and let her do whatever she wanted to do. It wasn't like him to meddle in other people's lives. Why should he care if she didn't believe the doctors? She'd learn soon enough that her knee was always going to give her trouble. A few pratfalls onstage, and she'd be looking for other work. She wouldn't have a choice. It wasn't his job to protect her, to show her she had options. He had his own plan to work on, the plan that was two-thirds fulfilled. He had the land and the house.

Now all he needed was the woman.

The music stopped, and he dropped his arms and backed away from her. "That's enough for today. I have something to show you."

"You do? What?"

"You'll see. Come on." He took her by the hand and pulled her along behind him.

She dug in her heels. "Where? What's going on?"

"To your studio. I'm trying to show you—"

"The hay's gone!"

She raced ahead of him, but he caught up with her before she got out the back door. Holding her by her nape, he told her, "Slow down. Most of the hay's gone. Not all of it."

"Most?" She wiggled out of his grasp and looked at him over her shoulder. "Why isn't it all gone? What did you do with it, anyway? You said your barn wouldn't be ready for another month."

"I couldn't wait. I rented a shed a few miles from here." She raised an eyebrow, but he wasn't about to explain why he'd wasted good money on hay storage. She didn't need to know he lusted after her. He put his hand on the small of her back and pushed. "Are you going or not?"

"I'm going. I just don't understand why you're so hot and bothered all of a sudden."

"I am not hot and bothered. I *am* in a hurry. I've wasted enough time this morning, and I want to get on with my plans for the day. Move, woman!"

She moved. When they got to the studio, he opened the door slowly. "Take it slow and easy," he whispered sternly. "We don't want to scare them again. They've just now settled down from all the commotion when we were taking the bales out of here."

"Scare who? Who—or what's—in here?" Sidonie whispered back, her eyes wide.

Rafe pointed to the remaining pile of hay, where a mother cat and two kittens nestled.

"Oh, look, aren't they sweet?" Sidonie sat down on the floor, her bad leg stuck out in front of her. "Did you feed them?"

"We gave Momma a dish of cream. She's taking care of the kittens for now."

"How old do you think they are?"

"Three or four weeks, I'd say. They've got their eyes open."

"Can I pick them up?"

"Go slow, and she'll probably let you. She doesn't act like a feral cat—probably a house cat someone dumped when she turned up pregnant."

"Dumped! Just like Gypsy. How can people do that? Take a sweet puppy or kitten into their home, then, as soon as they aren't c-convenient anymore, throw them away." She looked up at him, her blue eyes misty with unshed tears. "Think how scared she must have been. Poor baby," she crooned softly. "And she's so pretty, too. A calico, orange and black and white. One black-and-white kitten, and one orange tabby. Are they boys or girls?"

Rafe knelt down next to her, drawn by her warmth and his inexplicable need to comfort her. "The tabby's a female, and the black kitten's a male." He picked up the little tomcat, cuddled it in his hand and used one large finger to rub the kitten's back.

Sidonie watched him as she petted and stroked the

mother cat. "Aren't they adorable? Can you hear Momma purring? Have you named them yet?"

He rolled his eyes. "Nope. Naming animals is your job." Rafe gently put the kitten back at his mother's side. He glanced around the room.

"You were right—this is not a chicken coop. Buck did a really nice job on your studio."

"Yes, he did."

"It's bigger than it looks from the outside, too. You could hold classes in here." His not-so-subtle suggestion fell on deaf ears.

"I'm not a teacher."

"You're teaching me."

"That's different. I owe you."

"For what?"

"Letting me stay. Giving me a job—one I was barely qualified for." She waved her arms. "For this. Cleaning out the studio weeks before you had to."

"You don't owe me anything," he said gruffly. "As for cleaning out the studio, that was pure self-defense. I wanted you out of the house."

"Oh. Was the music bothering you?"

"Not the music. You."

"Me? What did I do?"

Taking her chin in his hand, he turned her face toward the mirror.

"Look at you."

She peered at her image. "Oh. I get it. Holes in my tights, my hair going every which way—not to mention sweaty and stinky. I'm a mess. No doubt about it—I destroy the ambience of your abode."

That wasn't the problem at all, but if she couldn't see that she was as adorable as the kittens, and sexy as all get-out to boot, he wasn't going to tell her. He frowned, registering her last remark. "Ambience? Where'd you get that?"

"From your decorator. She came by the house yesterday. Didn't I tell you?" She slanted a look at him, a look he should have recognized.

He shook his head. "No. You didn't mention it."

"Well, she was here, and I'm not kidding. She actually uses words like *ambience* and *abode*."

"She came to the house? Why? Was she looking for me? I told her I'd be at my place, checking out the progress on the barn."

"She wasn't looking for you. She was looking for clues. Apparently she needs to know a lot about you before she can choose the perfect chair and coffee table for Chez McMasters. And you're no help, because you never tell anyone anything personal, so she came to me. You know what they say—no one has any secrets from his housekeeper." She gave him a saucy wink.

"Elise asked you about me?"

Sidonie nodded, changing from flirtatious to solemn in the blink of an eye. "Who better? I told her she wouldn't be able to tell much about you from this house because you rented it already furnished. But don't worry, I gave her the complete lowdown on Rafe McMasters."

His stomach knotted. Sidonie and Elise had talked about him? Good Lord! "What did you tell her?"

"I showed her your closet—all those power suits arranged by season and color coordinated with your shirts and ties. From that we deduced that you are organized and outwardly conservative—not to mention rich enough to pay her fee."

"Conservative?"

"Outwardly. But I knew you'd want your decorator to have the whole picture, so I gave her a peek at your underwear drawer. Any man who has leopardskin briefs has hidden depths. I showed her your study, too."

Rafe felt himself getting light-headed. "My underwear drawer?" he said faintly. "My study?"

"Only from the door. We didn't enter your private sanctum. But she saw enough to confirm that you want the world to see you as a dull, stodgy businessman, not as a hell-raising cow—"

"This is a joke, right? Miss Prescott wasn't even here yesterday. Was she?"

"She was. Cross my heart and hope to die." Sidonie matched her actions to her words, tracing a cross over her left breast. "Shouldn't I have let her in? I was only trying to help you out. Maybe I shouldn't have showed her your collection of animal skin briefs, but don't worry. She told me she's not going to dwell on your playful side—I told her it was a *very* small part of the whole man. Just a hint or two here and there in the accessories. She mentioned a stuffed giraffe dressed in chaps and boots for the den, but, not to worry, the primary *ambience* will be traditional and conservative. The two of us agreed she couldn't go wrong if she stuck with the Victorian era. All that dark, heavy furniture would suit your stuffy—oops, sorry, that just slipped out—your conventional personality just fine."

"Victorian? I hate Victorian. I've got to call her." He jumped to his feet.

Sidonie grabbed him around the ankle before he could make it to the door. "Wait. Help me up."

He pulled her up next to him. She took his chin in

her hand and turned his face to the mirror. "Look at you—that horrified expression is priceless." She fell into his arms, laughing uncontrollably.

Rafe shut his eyes briefly. She'd done it again. "You were lying. She wasn't here."

"Exaggerating. She was here, but only to drop off some swatches. I didn't tell or show her anything."

He gave her a little shake. "You swear?"

She nodded, wiping the tears from her eyes. "I'm s-sorry." She hiccuped, swallowing her laughter, or trying to. "I couldn't help myself. You're so easy to tease!"

"Aw, hell. I can't help myself, either," he muttered, right before he hauled her into his arms and clamped his mouth on hers. Only to shut her up, he thought, even though he made it a practice never to lie to himself. Right now he needed the lie.

He had to at least try not to want her. She wasn't the right woman for him. He knew it, and she knew it. So why were her arms winding tighter around his neck? Why was she standing on her toes, *en pointe* he'd heard her call it, bringing her soft, full breasts into close contact with his chest? And why was she kissing him back?

With a groan he gave up the lie. He wanted more than her silence, a lot more. Rafe deepened the kiss, thrusting his tongue into her mouth, almost losing control completely when she made a soft, purring sound deep in her throat and pressed closer.

He forced himself to pull back—mentally, anyway. He couldn't quite manage letting go of her. Not yet. Nor could he stop kissing her. But it didn't mean anything. This was only a momentary lapse, not a complete capitulation.

Rafe had known exactly what he wanted for fifteen years. It would take more than a few hot kisses from a redheaded chorus girl to make him swerve from the course he'd set for himself.

But fate, and a sexy redhead, seemed hell-bent on giving him the opportunity to indulge in one last adventure before he settled down, one last taste of forbidden fruit. Sidonie seemed more than willing to go along with anything he wanted to do with her. Why shouldn't he take what she was offering?

He leaned over her, pressing her back against his arm. Her body arched gracefully, as he'd known it would, bringing her breasts within reach of his hungry mouth. She moaned as he closed his mouth over the tip of one silver-covered mound.

"Oh, Rafe," she moaned. If he was doing this to get even with her for teasing him, she'd kill him. But not yet, not just yet. Rafe replaced his mouth with his hand on her breast, stroking her like he'd stroked the kitten. She could purr for him, too, and she would, as soon as she caught her breath. But his mouth was on hers again, hot and demanding, and she couldn't waste time breathing. She had better things to do. Like kiss him back. Like unbutton his shirt, so she could touch hot, naked skin.

The sound of car doors slamming forced Sidonie to open her eyes.

Rafe hadn't heard. He was holding her tight against him, both hands on her bottom, kneading her derriere. His mouth was still working its magic.

"Yoo-hoo! Anybody home?"

His head jerked up. "Damn. Who could that be?"

"It sounded like Maggie."

Rafe let her go. Quickly changing gears, he said.

"I'll leave you two alone. I've got things to do." He strode out of the studio, headed in the direction of the barn.

Sidonie stood in the doorway, her mouth open in shock. She swayed a little. "Not steady on your feet, hmm? And why is that? Not because Mr. Pompous just kissed you silly, surely. Didn't bother him. He just walked away." She grabbed the towel she'd hung on the barre and scrubbed her face. If she was red all over, maybe Maggie wouldn't notice her swollen lips and flushed cheeks.

"Hello!" she called out. "I'm back here!"

Maggie and another woman came around the back of the house. "Sidonie! Why are you out here? The sky is blue and the temperature is in the seventies for the first time in weeks. How can you stand to stay cooped up on a gorgeous day like today?"

"Cooped up?" Sidonie smiled. "I hope that pun was intended."

"Couldn't resist. This is Cathy Sue Nicholls. She wanted to meet you."

Sidonie stuck out her hand. So this was the paragon, the model for Rafe's ideal woman. Naturally he'd omitted telling her that Cathy Sue was gorgeous. *Pretty* was the word he'd used. It didn't begin to describe soft blond hair upswept in an elegant chignon, huge hazel eyes rimmed in gold, smooth skin the color of pale champagne. A real golden girl.

Sidonie suddenly wished she weren't wearing her oldest leotard, a dismal pale gray color, except where it was dark with sweat. Her hair was pulled back in a haphazard ponytail, and she hadn't bothered with makeup. And she was still shaken from Rafe's kisses, angry at his abrupt departure. In short, she was not in the mood for company.

"How do you do?" Cathy Sue murmured, her voice soft, her accent more Southern syrup than Texas twang.

"Fine. I'm doing fine."

"How's the knee?" Maggie asked.

"Coming along." She couldn't take her eyes off Cathy Sue. "Why don't we go to the house? I'll fix us some iced tea."

"We came to see your dance studio, if you don't mind," Cathy Sue said.

"My studio?" Sidonie stepped back and let Maggie and Cathy Sue enter. "It's not cleaned up yet. Rafe just moved the hay out today."

"My! This really is a studio." Ignoring the cats, Cathy Sue clicked across the floor in her tasteful beige pumps. "Mirrors and a barre. I am impressed."

"Take off your shoes," Sidonie said. "Please," she added, in a grudging attempt to change her order to a request. Being around Cathy Sue was making her hackles rise, but there was no need to be rude.

Cathy Sue slipped off her shoes. "Oh dear, I left marks. You know what will take those right out? Rub vigorously with a fine steel wool pad and a good floor cleaner. Wipe dry, polish, and *voilà!* Good as new."

"Thanks, I'll try that." In a pig's eye.

"Once that last bale of hay is moved out, you'll be ready to go. Why was there hay in here, anyway?" asked Maggie.

"Rafe was storing a few bales in here until they finished his barn. But he found another place for it, and he moved it out this morning. All except for this one. See the kittens? Aren't they cute?"

"You'll have to get rid of them," Cathy Sue said.
"Put them in a gunnysack with a few rocks and drop
it in the river."

Sidonie gasped. "I will not!"

Cathy Sue shrugged. "Take them to Dr. Jones, then.
He'll put them down, if you're too squeamish to do it
yourself. The point is, cats multiply like rabbits. Keep
the adult around as a mouser, if you want, but if you
don't get rid of the kittens, before you know it you'll
be overrun." She brushed a stalk of hay off her skirt.
"That's my advice."

Sidonie sat down on the hay bale, putting her body
between Cathy Sue and the kittens. "I don't think I'll
take it." She caught Maggie's eye and raised an eyebrow.

Maggie rolled her eyes. "About the studio—"

"Yes, that's why we're here, isn't it? Not to give
lectures on animal husbandry." Kneeling gracefully,
Cathy Sue picked up her pumps and then strolled
around the room, carefully avoiding the hay bale.
"You could have several pupils in a class, couldn't
you? At least four or five."

"Class? What kind of class? What are you talking
about? Maggie, what's she talking about?"

"Dance classes. We thought maybe you were
ready—"

"No way! I am not a teacher. I am a dancer!"

"But Rafe said you're giving lessons," Maggie
said, looking bewildered.

"Rafe told you that?"

"Actually, he told me," Cathy Sue said. "We had
lunch together a day or two ago."

Sidonie's temper clicked up a notch. The son of a
gun hadn't said a thing to her about lunching with

Cathy Sue. How dare he kiss her like he meant it, then walk out, leaving her to deal with his old flame? "Private lessons. As a favor to him," she said silkily.

"But since he didn't need dance lessons, we naturally thought you were only doing it for practice. Although ballroom dancing isn't the same thing as ballet, I suppose the teaching techniques are the same."

"What makes you think Rafe doesn't need lessons?"

"He knows how to dance. He's a very good dancer."

"He does now—he learned fast. Did the two of you go dancing after lunch?"

Cathy Sue laughed. Her laugh sounded like a crystal wind chime. "How droll! Imagine Rafe and me dancing at the Pecan Café, Maggie. Wouldn't that have set the tongues to wagging?" She smiled a perfect smile at Sidonie. "Our lunch wasn't planned, dear. I was there alone. Rafe came in, and I couldn't resist asking him to join me. It was wicked of me, I know. The retired teachers were having their monthly luncheon meeting, and you know how some of those old... ladies talk. I just wanted to show them there were no hard feelings."

"Aren't there?" murmured Sidonie.

"Not at all. I forgave Rafe for deserting me years ago. I finally got the chance to tell him so, and I took it. Now, about lessons. My daughter—"

"I don't plan on giving lessons. Except to Rafe."

"But he doesn't need them. I taught him how to dance, years ago. Among other things. I had to. Poor boy never had done anything but that awful Texas two-step until I took him in hand. By the time of my senior prom, he danced like a dream." She paused and slanted a thoughtful look at Maggie. "I always thought dancing was like riding a bicycle—once learned, never forgotten. But I suppose if a man didn't dance for years and years, he might need a refresher course."

Sidonie rolled the towel up and draped it around her neck. It was either that, or use the towel to throttle Cathy Sue. Jilted or not, she obviously thought that Rafe had never gotten over her. "That must be it. What other things?"

"Excuse me?"

"You said you taught him other things, besides dancing."

Cathy Sue blushed prettily. She did everything prettily, it seemed. Sidonie tightened her grip on the ends of the towel.

"Rafe was something of a diamond in the rough back then," said Cathy Sue. "He didn't know how to dress, which fork to use at a formal dinner, how to make polite conversation."

"And you taught him all that?"

"Let's just say I exposed him to another way of life. As you said, he's a fast learner."

Sidonie smiled. "Yes, he is. And a fast worker, too."

Cathy Sue's eyes narrowed slightly. "What is that supposed to mean? Are you implying that something is going on between you two?"

"Implying? Listen, Mrs. Nicholls—"

"How large is the studio?" Maggie interjected, looking anxious.

"Twenty by twenty-four," said Sidonie. "Why?"

"Maybe four or five pupils wouldn't be enough for this to be a paying proposition for you, Sidonie."

"That's no problem," said Cathy Sue. "If she

needed to hold larger classes, I'm sure I could arrange for her to use the country club dance floor. There are even mirrors, behind the bandstand." She turned to Sidonie. "And you could buy some of those portable barres. I know I've seen them somewhere."

"Mrs. Nicholls, perhaps you didn't hear me before. I said I am not a teacher."

"Call me Cathy Sue. I heard you. Maggie, isn't it admirable that she is so candid about her lack of experience? But you've danced for so many years—and Rafe said you were an excellent teacher. Once people hear that my little Darcy is one of your students—well, I don't want to brag, but my endorsement is all you'll really need to get your business off the ground."

"Darcy is Elizabeth's best friend," explained Maggie. "And they're both dying to be ballerinas. Even if it's only temporary, couldn't you give them a few lessons? Maybe once they see how much hard work is involved, it will lose some of its glamour."

Sidonie caught a glimpse of herself in the mirror. Hot and sweaty, her knee throbbing, her head pounding. And there was a distinct ache in the vicinity of her heart. "Ah, glamour!" She sighed dramatically, striking a pose. "How I miss it."

Rafe chose that moment to return. "Ladies," he said warily, staring at Sidonie.

"Rafe!" cooed Cathy Sue, taking his arm and looking up at him adoringly. "I was hoping I'd get to see you."

"I'll just bet you were," muttered Sidonie.

"What have you been talking about?" he asked innocently.

"You'll never guess in a million years." Sidonie took the towel from around her neck and began twirling it. "Somehow Maggie and Cathy Sue got the idea I wanted to be a dance teacher. I was just telling them how wrong they are. I won't be here long enough for even a few lessons. Sorry, Maggie."

"Well, then, that's that," Cathy Sue said, holding on to Rafe as she slipped on her pumps. "But since I got to see you, the trip here wasn't a total waste. Walk me to the car, won't you?" She actually batted her eyes at him.

She gave both Maggie and Sidonie a gracious smile. It reminded Sidonie of an alligator's grin.

"Give me a few minutes before you come, will you, Maggie? I have something to discuss with Rafe. Something private." As they started out the door, Cathy Sue called out, "Oh, nice meeting you, Sidonie. I've heard so much about you. And your mother."

Sidonie snapped the towel, missing Rafe's backside by a hair. Cathy Sue looked over her shoulder, obviously puzzled. "What was that?"

"A pest," said Rafe, scowling at Sidonie. "I'll take care of it later."

"I wanted to talk to you about the Spring Dance. I know you planned to go alone, but I'd be more than happy to find you the perfect date..." Her voice faded away.

"You were right, Sidonie," said Maggie as they stood in the doorway watching Rafe and Cathy Sue walk away. "We really ought to shoot her."

Chapter Six

Sidonie lingered in the studio after Maggie left, playing with the kittens and trying to cool off. Her temper was still simmering when Rafe reappeared, carrying a wicker laundry basket.

"What's that for?"

"The cats. I'm moving them out of here. As soon as they're gone, we'll get rid of this last bale of hay and you'll be in business." He smoothed the blanket folded in the bottom of the basket and picked up the cat.

"Oh, no, I won't! I am not opening a dance studio."

"Did I say you were?" Scooping up both kittens, he put them in the basket with their mother.

"I'll be in business!" she said, mimicking him.

"Only a figure of speech," he said mildly, stroking the kittens, murmuring soft nonsense words to settle them down.

Those tactics wouldn't work on her. Not that she wanted his hands on her body or his voice whispering silly suggestions in her ears—of course she didn't want that. Dragging her eyes away from his hands, she lifted her gaze to his mouth. Big mistake. Remembering his kiss turned her knees to water and left her feeling disoriented.

She didn't want to let go of her anger, but she could feel it fading fast, leaving her vulnerable to his charms. Now was not the time to be weak and vulnerable. She had to be strong or she'd find herself...falling in love?

No! That couldn't be what was happening. All right, so Rafe's kisses made her dizzy, and his tender care of small, helpless creatures gave her the warm fuzzies—that didn't mean he was the man of her dreams. She didn't have dreams like that, about building a life together with one special man.

And it was for sure she didn't fit in his long-term plans. *Respectable? Docile?* Just remembering his silly list should be enough to keep her fuming for weeks, never mind that he'd tricked her into giving him lessons he didn't need. Squaring her shoulders, she forced herself to glare at him. "You told your old girlfriend I was going to teach dancing. You lied."

"No. She asked, and I told her I thought you might decide to teach, once you faced facts. Let's get the cats out of here." Rafe picked up the laundry basket and walked past her, headed for the door.

She grabbed his arm, suddenly anxious. A small creek ran through her property, only a few yards behind the barn. "Where are you taking them?" Surely Rafe did not agree with Cathy Sue's method of feline population control.

"To the house. The utility room is warm and dry. I don't think Gypsy will object, do you?"

"You're not going to drown them?"

He shot her a surprised look. "Good grief, no. What gave you that idea?"

"Your old girlfriend said that was the thing to do, or we'd be overrun with cats." She let go of his arm and followed him out of the studio, closing the door behind them. "Which reminds me, Cathy Sue said some other things, too. Things you need to explain."

"Cathy Sue has a big mouth."

"No kidding." At least he recognized the paragon had a few flaws. "I should have given her a fat lip to go with it."

"What did she say?"

"That she taught you to dance years ago. Is that true?"

He put his head down and mumbled something. Something that sounded more like a curse than a denial.

"She did, didn't she? You knew how to dance all along—and you stepped on my toes! On purpose, just so I'd believe you." She made a fist and hit him on the shoulder. "You did lie! Why?"

Rafe set the basket down next to the clothes dryer. Rubbing his shoulder as if she'd really hurt him, he said, "It seemed like a good idea at the time. The doctor said you could handle that kind of dancing. I wanted you to see you have choices."

"I don't need choices. I know what I want."

"Sometimes we can't have what we want, and we have to settle for something else."

"I'm not settling for anything. My knee's getting stronger every day." Sidonie stalked into the kitchen with Rafe right behind her.

"I'm sorry. I had no right to tell Cathy Sue you

might be interested in teaching little girls how to dance.''

Somewhat mollified, Sidonie asked, ''Why were you talking about me, anyway? I would have thought the two of you would have better things to do.'' She moved to the counter and reached for the coffeepot.

''Yeah? Like what?'' Rafe took the coffee canister from the pantry shelf and handed it to her.

''Old times. Instead you talked about me. I hate being talked about behind my back. I thought you did, too.''

''I didn't bring you up. Cathy Sue wanted to know about you. About us, I should say.''

''I bet she did,'' Sidonie muttered as she measured the coffee into the filter. She winced. Rafe had been afraid people would jump to conclusions about their relationship. And she'd promised to make it clear that there was nothing between them.

''I had to tell her something. Talking about your studio was the first thing that came to mind. And then one thing led to another....'' Frowning, he trailed off. Catching her disbelieving eye on him, he blustered, ''I don't make a practice of sticking my nose in other people's business.''

''No? Then how did I get so lucky?''

''Darned if I know. Maybe it's self-defense. You're pretty good at sticking your nose in where it's not wanted.''

''Don't put the blame on me. I haven't told anyone anything about you. And I'm sure there are loads of people who'd pay me to tell what I do know. Like where you've been for the past fifteen years, for instance. No, I'm not nearly as interfering as you are. I think you owe me an apology.''

"Apology!" Rafe's face reddened and he puffed out his cheeks. For a second she thought he was going to explode. Then he let out the breath he'd been holding in a whoosh. Not meeting her gaze, he said, "You're right. I'm sorry."

Sidonie smothered a grin. Not the most gracious apology, but she could tell he was sincere. She had no reason not to accept it, except...for the first time, he seemed off balance and unsure of himself. She hated to waste an opportunity. "Maybe you are, and maybe you aren't. But you owe me more than a reluctant 'sorry.'"

"I don't owe you a thing."

"Yes, you do. I don't want much. Nothing immoral or illegal. All you have to do is answer a few questions. It's only fair. You and Cathy Sue talked about me. Now let's talk about you." She sat down at the kitchen table. "Have a seat."

"What kind of questions?" he asked warily as he took the chair opposite her.

"For starters—do you regret jilting Cathy Sue?"

He closed his eyes, then opened them again, narrowly. "Nope."

She waited a beat. He just looked at her. "Don't start with that Gary Cooper imitation. 'Nope' and 'yep' aren't going to cut it. You have to tell me why you have no regrets. Isn't Cathy Sue the model for your perfect woman?"

"If she'd been everything I wanted, I wouldn't have left her, would I?"

"Oh. I hadn't looked at it that way. I thought maybe you didn't know what you wanted—until you'd walked away from it."

"I knew. I wanted the same things then that I do

now—my own place, my own woman, a family. The difference is, now I'm ready for them.''

"And you weren't when you were twenty?''

"I thought I was. I found out different.''

He got up and filled two mugs with the freshly brewed coffee. Sidonie was surprised he was answering her questions, even cryptically. He must really feel bad about poking his nose in her business. How much more could she pry out of him before he got over his guilt attack?

"Tell me about it,'' she prodded.

He didn't answer right away. Instead, he took his time, adding cream and sugar to one of the mugs, then carrying both to the table. He handed the mug to her. "Why do you want to know?''

"Why, Rafe, don't you know how fascinating you are?'' She batted her eyes and made her voice drip honey. "Why do you think everyone wants to know what you've been up to for the past fifteen years? Mostly because you won't tell them. You've created a mystery, and now you get touchy when people want to solve it. There is a solution to your problem, however.''

"Oh, yeah? What would that be?''

"Simple. Tell me, I'll spread it around, and no one will bother you anymore.''

"No one is bothering me now. Except you. And you've known for weeks that I ended up in Chicago working for Cornelius Fielding. That didn't save me from this inquisition.''

"Well, of course it didn't. I don't know how you ended up in Illinois, working for a billionaire. Corny said you saved his life, but I couldn't tell if he meant that literally. Did he?''

"That's the way he sees it. But the truth is, I only kept him from being kidnapped. I don't think they would have killed him. They needed him alive to collect the ransom." He brought the coffee mug to his lips and took a swallow, eyeing her over the rim.

"Oh, no. You're not getting away that easy. Go on. Tell me the rest."

With a resigned sigh he set the cup down. "Not much to tell. After I left here, I drifted north. I ended up in Wisconsin, broke, looking for a job. Cornelius kept a few horses on a farm in Door County, and he had advertised for a stable hand. I stumbled into the kidnapping attempt and managed to get the drop on one of the kidnappers, the driver. He was waiting in a van for the other two to bring Corny from the house. When they arrived, they put Corny in the back of the van, and I took off before they had a chance to climb in after him. Not much to it, really. But Corny was grateful, and he gave me a job."

Sidonie knew that Rafe's dry recital was only the bare bones of the story. He was leaving out important details, like what he'd done to the driver and whether shots had been fired at the van as he and Corny made their escape. But she could let her imagination fill in those blanks. She wanted to know about Rafe.

"He hired you as a stable hand?"

"No. As a bodyguard." He tried to hide a sly grin behind the mug. "Turned out there was an opening for one."

"I guess so. Somebody must have goofed up royally for the kidnappers to have gotten as far as they did."

He shrugged and took another sip of coffee.

She looked at the expensive gold watch on his wrist,

exposed as he lifted the mug to his lips. "Guarding bodies must pay well."

"My duties expanded as Corny and I got to know each other better."

"He said something else..." She frowned, trying to remember. "Oh, yes. He said he taught you about commodity trading. Isn't that kind of risky?"

"Only if you can't afford to lose. That lesson I had to learn on my own. I took risks before I was ready and lost my shirt—more than once. But I only lost everything the first time. After that I sat down and made a plan. I decided I would always hold back twenty percent of whatever was in my pot—enough to start over if I lost big again. And every time I hit it big, I put another twenty percent aside to buy land."

"You had a plan, and you've executed it. You must feel very proud."

"I'm not finished yet. I have one more goal to reach."

"Oh, yes. Finding Miss Perfect."

"I'm not looking for the perfect woman. Only the right one."

"No? Cathy Sue is good-looking, rich and she wins prizes at the County Fair. If you overlook the fact that she drowns helpless little kittens, she's almost perfect. Why isn't she right for you?" She almost added "not docile enough?" but she held her tongue. He'd stop answering her questions if he knew she'd snooped.

"She's married."

"She wasn't married fifteen years ago. Why did you dump her?"

He set the empty mug down with a thump. "That's enough. No more questions from you. Now it's my turn. What are you going to do with the rest of your life? Have you made a plan?"

"Sure."

"Well? What is it?"

"Uh…well, I'm going to get in shape, then I'm going to go to a few auditions and…see what turns up," she concluded with a triumphant grin.

"That's it?"

"It's a plan."

"It's a disaster. You're putting all your eggs in one basket. You haven't set up any alternatives, in case of setbacks or failure."

She stuck out her chin. "I don't intend to fail."

"That's not the point. Planning for the worst doesn't mean it's going to happen. Knowing you've got something to fall back on increases your chances of success—it makes you more confident."

"Do I strike you as someone lacking in confidence?" she asked, with more bravado than true confidence. Sidonie squirmed uncomfortably in her chair. What he was saying was beginning to make sense.

"While you're waiting around to see what turns up, why don't you give some thought to ranching? You've got a nice little spread here. Good, reliable water supply, good fences and plenty of open pasture. You could run a small herd of cattle or raise sheep like your dad. You'd only need one or two hands to run the place. I could have my men help out until you—"

"Hold it! You're doing it again—interfering, deciding what I should do with the rest of my life. It's not your problem."

"You're right about that. I should shut up and let you fall flat on your pretty face. But I can't do that. You've got to face facts—you've got problems."

"My only problem is my knee. Once it's better, everything will be fine."

"For a while, maybe. But even if your knee recovers one hundred percent, you can't dance forever."

"I know. I'll worry about that when the time comes."

"Don't you ever plan ahead?"

"No. Don't you ever do anything spontaneous?" she snapped, tired of his criticism. Immediately she remembered the kiss. That hadn't been planned, she was sure. She jerked her gaze from his mouth to his eyes. They'd darkened from chocolate to ebony. He was remembering the kiss, too.

"Now and then," he admitted, scowling at her mouth. "Usually I'm sorry afterward."

He regretted kissing her. That smarted. "Well, don't do it again."

"Don't worry, I won't."

"Good."

"Right."

They stared at each other for a few heartbeats.

"Sell this place to me," he said abruptly.

"What? I will not." Maybe she'd misjudged him. That was the second spontaneous thing he'd done today.

"Why not? You'd make more taking the money and investing it than you ever will leasing the grazing rights."

"I don't need much money."

"I could use the land and the house. I hired another hand last week, and he's getting married soon. He'll be needing a house."

"Well, he can't have this one. It's mine. And it's not for sale."

"You're never going to live here."

"I may. Someday."

"When?"

"When I get good and ready. Will you drop it, please?"

"Not yet."

Good grief. Now that she'd gotten him talking, he didn't want to stop. She'd created a monster.

"What are you doing next week?" he asked. "Or haven't you planned that far ahead?"

"I don't know. Cooking, cleaning, working out. Same thing I'm doing this week."

"No doctor appointments scheduled? No auditions?"

"No. Why?"

"Go with me to San Antonio. The rodeo and livestock show will be opening this weekend. How long has it been since you've been to a rodeo?"

"Years. Not since Daddy died."

"It's time you went again. It is part of your heritage, after all, and it can be almost as exciting as Broadway."

"What about Tequila, Baby and Gypsy? Not to mention Jasmine and Magnolia and Zorro? We can't leave them alone."

"Who are Jasmine and Mag—oh, you named the cats. Zorro?"

"I couldn't think of a flower name for a male. And he does have that mask."

"I'll have Joe Moody—he's my foreman—come by a couple of times a day to feed and water your menagerie."

She eyed him suspiciously. "This isn't a date, is it?"

"Lord, no. This is a field trip for you, a business trip for me. You can learn about ranching, and I can check out different breeds of cattle."

She could feel herself weakening. A little voice was trying to tell her taking a trip with Rafe was not a good idea, but she ignored it. "San Antonio was always one of my favorite places. Can we take a boat ride on the river? I mean, even though it's not a date, it is all right to have some fun, isn't it?"

"Sure. I'm not as stuffy as you make me out to be." He gave her a wicked grin. "If you really want to have fun, we can share a room."

First he'd talked, now he was teasing her. She *had* created a monster! "Well, gee, thanks. But no, thanks. I couldn't take that much excitement." She stuck her nose in the air. "Besides, I am not that kind of girl."

What kind of girl was Sidonie Saddler? Rafe slanted a glance at the woman sitting next to him in the car. He'd thought he'd known exactly what type she was— definitely not his—the first time he met her. But now he wasn't so sure. She still wasn't right for him, but she was full of surprises.

They were almost at San Antonio, and she was getting more excited by the minute. He'd have thought it was because they were headed for the bright lights of a big city, if she hadn't spent the whole trip telling him stories about every rodeo she'd ever been to.

Any reluctance she'd felt about going with him to the annual San Antonio Livestock Exposition and Rodeo had been replaced by mind-boggling enthusiasm. She wanted to do everything—go to the rodeo, see a country-western music concert, visit all the displays of tractors and windmills, watch the judging of the various breeds of cattle, sheep and goats. Even with her bad knee, he could tell he might have trouble keeping up with her.

"Where are we staying?" she asked.

"At the Casa del Rio. In separate rooms."

She raised an eyebrow. "I should hope so. Casa del Rio. Is it on the river? Don't you love the San Antonio River? I do—the way it winds through town, all lazy and slow, oblivious to the hustle and bustle on its banks. Do they still have those paddleboats? When can we take a ride?"

He grinned. "Yes, the hotel is on the river. We can rent a paddleboat as soon as we get there, if you want to. Nothing's going on at the livestock show until tomorrow morning."

"And can we go to La Margarita for Mexican food tonight? I haven't had fajitas in ages."

"Yes." Sidonie's enthusiasm was catching. Rafe found himself looking forward to the evening. No matter what Sidonie said, it was beginning to look like a date to him. And a date meant a good-night kiss. Or two or three.

"What are you grinning about?" she asked suspiciously.

"Nothing in particular. I just feel good."

The feeling didn't last. Sidonie treated him like a long-lost brother all evening. He was the only man she'd kept at a distance, however. She'd flirted with the guy who rented them the paddleboat, then with the waiter, the maître d' and all three mariachis at the restaurant.

By the time they returned to the hotel, he was in a foul mood.

"Good night, Rafe," she told him when they got to

her door. "I know it wasn't a real date, but I had a wonderful time."

"Tell me about it," he snarled. "You entertained half the male population of San Antonio."

She pulled herself up and gave him a haughty stare. "Excuse me? What put you in a snit?"

"Snit? This isn't a *snit*. I don't even know what a snit is. I'm pissed."

"I can tell that," she said sharply. "*Why* is a puzzle, however."

"You acted like...like..."

"Like someone enjoying herself?" she ventured.

"Exactly! You were having *fun*."

"Well, Mr. Sour and Stuffy, you needn't make it sound like I committed a heinous sin." She fumbled in her purse and pulled out her room key card. Shoving it in the slot, she opened the door. "Good night!"

He pushed against the door, keeping her from closing it. She wasn't getting away that easily. "Wait just a damn minute. I have a few things to say to you."

She leaned into the door, blocking his entrance. "I don't want to hear them. You're all worked up to give me another lecture, and I'm not in the mood. I've put up with your criticism and your instructions and your *plans* for my life, because I thought it was kind of cute—the way you try to control everything in sight. I thought you meant well. You were changing, too—loosening up, learning to have—yes, I'm going to say it—*fun!*" She gave the door a shove, but he held it open.

"Sidonie—"

"Go away! Why did you have to go and r-ruin everything?"

"Aw, hell, Sidonie, I don't know why I'm acting like a jerk."

"Of course you don't. You'd never admit you were jealous, not even to yourself."

"Jealous? Over you?" Thunderstruck, he pushed his way into the room. "Where'd you get a fool idea like that?"

"It was obvious to everyone at the restaurant," she said smugly. "Especially after you almost got into a fight with the mariachis."

She was awfully sure of herself. But she couldn't be right. It wasn't jealousy that had him feeling meaner than a junkyard dog. She'd offended his sense of propriety, that's all. A lady would have devoted all her attention to her escort, not to every other male who happened along.

"You're wrong," he insisted. "Jealously implies...a certain level of involvement between two people. We're not involved."

"No? We're living together. But I guess that's not *involved.*"

Her lips were curved in that mischievous grin—the one that said she was teasing him again. A little demon that he'd thought he'd outgrown a long time ago told him to give her a taste of her own medicine.

Rafe closed the door behind him and moved farther into the room. Sidonie backed away from him, her smug grin slipping a little. "Maybe you're right. Maybe I was jealous. Come here, Sidonie."

"What for?" Her eyes narrowed, and the grin disappeared.

"A little test...to check our level of involvement."

"No. That won't be necessary. On second thought, you were right. We're only roommates. Temporarily.

We could not possibly be involved romantically. We don't have anything in common."

He moved closer, struggling to keep a serious expression on his face. "I wouldn't say that. We both like cats. And dogs."

"But not cows. You don't like cows." Sidonie bumped into the bed. She looked behind her, then took a step in his direction.

Rafe held his ground, but he didn't move closer. He didn't want to spook her. "Of course I like cows. Why would I want to spend the rest of my life raising cows—cattle—if I didn't like them?"

"But you kill them."

"Not personally. And not the cows. I keep the cows and sell the calves, some of them. And you eat them. What do you think was in those fajitas? It wasn't soy beans."

She looked stricken. "I ate steak. You're right. I have no business denouncing the way you choose to make a living."

"We have other things in common, too. We like to dance. I wanted to dance with you tonight, did you know that? I should have let you teach me to cha-cha. Then you could have danced with me instead of with the waiter."

"That was a rumba, not a cha-cha."

"Whatever. Are you going to let me kiss you goodnight?"

"Why? Tonight wasn't a date."

"No."

"Then why do you want to kiss me? Is that the test?"

He shook his head. "No test."

"Then why?"

"Just for fun. You said you liked to have fun." He closed the short distance between them and took her in his arms. Before she could come to her senses and tell him to get out of her room, he covered her mouth with his.

Fun? This was more than fun. It was A1, five-star, top-drawer, sheer, unadulterated pleasure. As her lips softened beneath his gentle assault, he tightened his hold on her. He never wanted to let her go. He couldn't remember feeling, wanting, needing so much—

No. There was such a thing as too much fun. This kind of fun could make him forget his goal, modify his plan. He tried to end the kiss, but Sidonie chose that moment to send her tongue on a sweet foray into his mouth.

A little longer. He'd have fun just a little longer. Sidonie's arms slid around his neck and she arched her body into his. With a muttered oath, Rafe told himself he had no choice—he followed her lead and deepened the kiss.

Chapter Seven

The telephone rang. Sidonie groped for the receiver. "Umm?" she managed to say, her eyes squeezed tightly shut.

"Morning, sweetness," drawled a sexy male voice.

"Who…'s it?" she slurred, slitting open one eye.

A deep, masculine chuckle came over the wire. "It's me. Wake up, little darlin'. It's time to get going."

"Rafe?" She pressed the receiver closer to her ear. "Go where? What time is it?"

"Six. Meet me in the lobby in fifteen minutes…or I'm coming to get you." That deliciously sensual threat was followed by a click and a dial tone.

Sidonie pried both eyes open and stared at the receiver. "Meet who in the lobby?" She hadn't been talking to Rafe. Rafe wouldn't call her names like "sweetness" and "little darlin'" in that husky drawl.

Unless…she'd been right all along, and he had been jealous last night. He'd never admitted it, but she had goaded him into kissing her again. And what a kiss! Sidonie touched her mouth with her fingertips, remembering. The memory sent tingles coursing through her nerve endings, chasing the last vestiges of sleepiness from her body and mind. Another minute of a kiss like that and she'd have forgotten she was only teasing him. She just might have done anything he wanted. But he'd ended the kiss abruptly and left without even saying good-night.

He'd remembered she wasn't his type. That's what she'd attributed his hasty exit to last night. But she could have been wrong. That phone call—was he coming back for more? Shoving the covers aside, she sat up and looked at the clock.

"Ohmigod! Did he say fifteen minutes? I've only got ten left."

Luckily she'd showered the night before. Sidonie slithered into blue tights and a short denim skirt the same shade of blue. She topped it off with the white cashmere sweater Belle had sent her from Ireland, and pulled on a pair of boots Buck had given her for her sixteenth birthday. A touch of blush and a dab of lip gloss and she was out the door with a minute to spare. She strolled off the elevator, the denim and boots making her feel like she'd fit right in with the country-western crowd. Rafe wouldn't, she thought with a smile. After months in Texas, he persisted in dressing like he was going to his office in a Chicago skyscraper.

Looking around the lobby, her glance slid over a tall cowboy lounging against a pillar. He was wearing well-worn jeans, snakeskin boots, and a wide leather belt with a silver buckle that proclaimed him a champion bronc buster. He pushed his black Stetson back off his forehead and Sidonie did a double take. The cowboy was Rafe!

He pushed away from the pillar and ambled toward her. "Howdy, pardner. Ready for breakfast?"

She could only nod. Rafe took her by the arm and led her out of the hotel. They started the day with *huevos rancheros* and strong coffee at a small restaurant on the river. Then he took her to the livestock show, where they looked at llamas and ostriches, goats and sheep and miniature horses.

Rafe quizzed the exhibitors about the pros and cons of raising the various animals, but he wasn't all business. He played, too, stroking the soft pelt of the llamas, petting the tiny horses. He definitely was in a playful mood. He might have filled her tote with literature, but he stuffed her mouth with cotton candy, hot dogs and ice-cold beer. In between visits to the various show rings, they hit the arcade, and Rafe won her a teddy bear at a shooting gallery. And all through the day, there were touches. He'd put his hand on her back, or taken her by the elbow to guide her through the crowd. A time or two he'd slid his arm around her waist, pulling her close to his side and out of harm's way when cattle were being moved through the wide aisles.

That evening they went to the rodeo and cheered the barrel racers, the bulldoggers and the bronc riders until they were hoarse. Then Rafe insisted that they stay for the country-western concert. He surprised her again by knowing the words to most of the songs. He proved it by singing along, his mouth next to her ear. Occasionally he stopped humming long enough to nibble on her ear.

When the last song had been sung at midnight, Sid-

onie was jumpy as one of the kittens they'd left in
Cache. She expected him to take her back to the hotel,
and the thought of being alone with him was filling
her with a strange combination of trepidation and
longing. But, to her amazement, their wonderful day
wasn't over yet. On the way out of the arena, Rafe
asked a bronc rider he knew from the old days where
the action was. Following the man's directions, they
ended up at a rowdy honky-tonk, complete with a live
band and a mechanical bull.

When they were seated at a small round table, Rafe
ordered two beers in long-neck bottles, then asked Sidonie to dance. The band was playing a slow ballad,
and the dance floor was crowded with couples moving
in time to the romantic music.

"Tonight you're dancing with me, not the waiter,"
he told her, as he led her onto the floor.

"We had a waitress."

Swinging her into his arms, he told her with mock
severity, "No dancing with other cowboys, then."

"Why, Mr. McMasters, are you the possessive
type?" she teased, trying to lighten the moment. She
had to do something to keep some distance between
them. Things were moving way too fast and in a totally unexpected direction.

"I am tonight." He sounded serious. And sexy.

Sidonie had a feeling she was in deep trouble. By
the time they were at her hotel room door, she was
sure of it.

She stuck out her hand. "Good night, Rafe. I
had...fun this evening."

Rafe took her hand and held on. "You sound surprised. Didn't think I knew how to have fun, did
you?"

"Well...no."

"You pegged me as stuffy from the beginning."

"I did. But I learned my lesson—you can't judge a book by its cover."

"I think I may have been wrong about you, too."

"Really? In what way?"

"I thought you weren't my type."

"Oh, you were right about that. I'm definitely not the woman for you."

"Maybe you're not the woman for me forever, but you sure seem like the right one for tonight." He pulled her into his arms and kissed her.

His kiss was whispery soft, not at all scary. She relaxed. Only a gentle kiss between friends. A quick, good-night kiss. She could handle that.

He ended the kiss, and she smiled at him. "Good night, Rafe."

"Not yet, sweetheart. One more time."

His head swooped down, and he kissed her again. This time there was nothing soft or gentle about the kiss. Hard, hot and demanding, he moved his mouth on hers.

Sidonie's toes curled in her boots. Heat seeped into her veins, and her lips softened like warm butter. She wound her arms around his neck and held on for dear life.

The next morning Sidonie gazed sleepily at Rafe as she sipped her coffee from a foam cup. He didn't seem any the worse for wear. Rafe appeared to be full of stamina and ready for their second and last day at the livestock show. Working for a billionaire must have involved more than pushing pencils and counting beans. He was in great shape.

After last night there was no doubt about it. Rafe knew how to show a girl a good time—as long as she didn't require eight hours sleep. When he'd left after that dynamite kiss, she'd been too restless to sleep. Yawning hugely, Sidonie tried to concentrate on the map of the exhibition area that Rafe had spread out on the counter of the snack bar.

"The Charolais are over there." Rafe stabbed a spot on the map with his finger. "Right next to the Beefmasters."

Sidonie pointed to another spot. "The potbellied pigs are in that direction."

"I'm a cattle rancher, not a pig farmer." He slid off his stool and stood behind her. Twirling her stool around, he put his hands on her waist and lifted her to the ground.

His hands stayed on her waist, kneading gently. Sidonie leaned into him, resting her cheek on his chest. "Well, I may be a pig farmer. I need to see what it would be like. But first I need to wake up." She yawned again.

"If you can't keep up, you should have stayed in bed." He reached for his coffee and held it to her lips. "Drink this."

She took a sip. "Ugh! It's black."

"Caffeine in its pure form. Drink up, it'll wake you up."

Pushing the cup away, Sidonie blinked her eyes. "I'm awake. Honest. And I want to see the potbellied pigs."

"We looked at ostriches, emus and llamas yesterday. Today, I'm looking at bulls."

He sounded like his old bossy self, but he was in

jeans and boots again this morning, still more cowboy than businessman.

"I don't want to look at cows. I know I don't want to be a cattle rancher, and I still haven't found anything else I want to raise. Ostriches and emus get killed for their feathers and their hides. Llamas are sweet, but expensive. You were right—all the exotics are overpriced and impractical." She slid her arms around his waist and looked at him. "But how much can a little bitty pig cost? And pigs are normal farm animals." She moved closer, backing him against the counter.

A gleam lit his dark eyes. She knew exactly what that meant. He wanted to kiss her. That woke her up. Thinking about kissing Rafe made her heart race and her breath quicken. She tickled his ribs, and he grabbed her hands.

"Potbellied pigs aren't normal. They're runts. You couldn't get a decent slab of bacon from one. They're nothing but pets."

"So? What do you have against pets?"

"Do you know how many you'd have to sell to make a living?"

"No. That's why I want to go over there and talk to people who do know."

Rafe took off his Stetson and shoved his hand through his hair and glowered at her. Sidonie grinned at him. She loved crossing him. He was so cute when he was exasperated. He replaced his hat. "All right. Look. When you're done, meet me here." He pointed to a place on the map. "We'll get something to eat before we head back to Cache."

A twinge of guilt made her momentarily uncomfortable. Rafe had said this was a business trip. With her urging him on, he'd succeeded in mixing a lot of pleasure with the business, but it was time to back off and give the man some breathing room. Sidonie rummaged through the stack of brochures, flyers and magazines Rafe had insisted she pick up at the various exhibits looking for her copy of the map of the exhibit hall. "Got it." She pulled the map out and located the spot Rafe had pointed to. "The food court? Okay. See ya."

"At noon, straight up. If you're late I'll leave without you."

He would not. She'd bet her tutu on that. Sidonie had learned a lot about Rafe in the two days they'd been at the livestock show. She watched him stride away. The man sure looked great in jeans and boots, even better than he did in his tailored suits. She ogled his rear until he walked through a group of schoolchildren and turned the corner, out of sight.

Checking the map for the location of the potbellied pigs, she began making her way through the crowds. As she dodged schoolchildren and tourists, cowboys and city slickers, she continued her catalog of Rafe's traits. She'd also learned that he wasn't nearly as pompous as he pretended to be. Rafe McMasters might not be a party animal, but he knew how to have fun.

The first night he'd only done what she'd insisted on—the boat ride on the river, dinner at La Margarita. Yesterday, however, had been all his idea. Spending the days at the livestock show had been the purpose of the trip, and attending the rodeo and the concert last night hadn't been completely unexpected. But the trip to the honky-tonk had shown her a whole new side of Rafe.

Remembering what had happened when he'd taken

her to her room last night had her fanning herself with the map. He'd taught her something else last night. His kisses got better and better.

When he'd kissed her before, he'd done it well, but she'd sensed that he was holding something back. Back in Cache, he'd kissed her because he was attracted to her—and because she'd teased him unmercifully—but he'd made it clear he didn't approve of her or her life-style. He might have wanted to kiss her, but it didn't mean anything.

But yesterday and last night, he'd been a different man. Not serious, not stuffy and not judgmental. He'd shown her the Rafe McMasters Maggie had mooned over and the judge had warned her about. That Rafe, and the way he'd kissed her last night, made a woman think about rearranging priorities, changing her ways.

Settling down.

Sidonie stopped abruptly. Settling down? Her? No way. It wasn't time to hang up her toe shoes yet. Her knee was improving steadily, and she was sure it would be one hundred percent recovered soon. A few hot kisses from a reluctant cowboy weren't enough to change her mind about what she wanted to do for the next few years.

Jostled by a family group headed in the opposite direction, Sidonie shook her head to get rid of the disturbing thoughts stirred up by her memories of Rafe's kisses. She looked around. She'd reached the area set aside for potbellied pigs. A large woman standing next to a pen smiled at her.

Sidonie smiled back, then looked in the pen. "Oh, look, aren't they precious?"

The pen held several tiny piglets, black, with little sagging bellies that almost touched the ground. The woman nodded. "Nothing cuter. Would you like to hold one?"

"Could I?"

The woman picked up one of the piglets and handed it to Sidonie. "They're very smart—smarter than dogs. And they can be housebroken. It's easy to train them to use a litter box just like a cat."

The piglet was trying to climb onto her shoulder. Sidonie held him closer to her face, and he nuzzled her neck.

"They're very affectionate, too," added the woman.

"I can tell. How big will he get?"

"Anywhere from thirty-five to fifty pounds—no larger than that."

Recalling why she was looking at pigs, Sidonie asked the woman about breeding and raising them. The woman enthusiastically explained more than she wanted to know about the subject. She paid attention to every word—somehow she knew Rafe would quiz her on it later.

Sidonie reluctantly gave the piglet back to its owner. "Thanks for the information. If I ever decide to raise pigs, I'll get in touch with you." She dutifully picked up a brochure from NAPPA, the North American Potbellied Pig Association.

As she strolled toward the food court, Sidonie found she hadn't rid herself of the settling-down idea. If it wouldn't go away, she'd have to let it run its course. Rafe's kisses aside, there were reasons to consider spending more time in Proffit County. No dancer's career lasted forever. Rafe had been right about that.

Maybe he'd been right about planning ahead, too. It would not hurt for her to think about her options. What would she do when the time came to move offstage and on to something else? Where would she be five years from now? Without a crystal ball, she didn't have a clue. Frowning, she tried again. First she'd eliminate the things she didn't want to do.

She had neither the talent nor the desire to become a choreographer like her mother. Once she was through with show business, she wanted to try something different. The trouble was, greasepaint and applause made for a hard act to follow. Whatever she chose had to be exciting. She couldn't see that teaching little girls how to plié and pirouette would generate much in the way of thrills.

Although, when she thought back, she could still feel the excitement of her first lessons—the delight when she'd mastered a new step, the pleasure of being praised for a graceful move. Maybe it wouldn't kill her to give a few lessons to Elizabeth and Darcy before she left Cache. Dancing had opened a whole new world for her. She owed it to her goddaughter—and her goddaughter's best friend—to give them a taste of what she'd experienced.

If it turned out that they loved dancing as much as she did and they really wanted to learn more after she left town, they could go to Dallas or Waco for lessons. Or Cathy Sue could use some of her big bucks to import a teacher for them. So maybe teaching wasn't completely out of the question.

But ranching definitely was. No matter what Rafe thought, she was too squeamish to deal with herds or flocks or gaggles of animals bound for slaughter. Sidonie knew it was hypocritical to eat burgers and balk at raising cattle for beef, but she couldn't help it. She liked animals, but she'd been raised a carnivore, and the only way she'd ever be a vegetarian would be if she had to personally kill her own meat. Short of that, she wanted to have her rib eye and eat it, too. But someone else would have to raise the cattle. It wouldn't be her.

She glanced at the brochure in her hand. Potbellied pigs on the other hand...

What was she thinking of? She didn't really want to be a pig farmer, no matter how cute the pigs were. So what was she going to do with her life after dance?

An image popped into her mind. She saw herself dressed in calico, in the kitchen of Rafe's hilltop house, surrounded by little boys and girls who looked exactly like Rafe McMasters, except for their flaming red hair.

Sidonie came to a complete stop, gripped by a sudden paralysis. She held her breath, terrified by the vivid image. What could that mean? Not that she wanted to spend the rest of her life with Rafe. He couldn't be the reason home and hearth were suddenly appealing. Jostled from behind by a group of young boys, Sidonie began walking again. She forced air into her lungs with a deep-breathing exercise until the image faded.

It wasn't Rafe. She'd had similar weird longings before she'd even met him—the night she'd found Gypsy. But her yearning for things she'd never had and never wanted had grown stronger, she realized. But why had she focused on Rafe?

His search for the perfect mate for the rest of his life must be the reason she'd thought of him in connection with the rest of hers. That was crazy. He wasn't right for her, even if he wasn't as stuffy as she'd thought he was before last night. She sure wasn't the right woman for him. He'd made that clear from the beginning. But why had he gotten jealous? And why had he shown her that he knew more than a little about having a good time?

Maybe he was having second thoughts about what he was looking for. The same kind of second thoughts that kept popping up in her mind.

Sidonie quickened her pace. She had to see Rafe as soon as possible. Surely if she came face-to-face with him, the fantasy would fade. Or grow clearer.

When she reached the food court, Rafe was in line at the barbecue stand. He was not alone. Cathy Sue and another woman were talking to him. Sidonie slowed down—she'd practically run the last few yards—and caught her breath. The unknown woman, a petite blonde, was wearing a blue calico dress.

Pasting a smile on her face, she joined the group. "Hi!" she said cheerily, although her stomach was suddenly in knots.

Rafe looked surprised to see her. He glanced at his watch. "I don't believe it. You're on time."

Why did she get the impression he'd been hoping she'd be late? And why should that hurt? "You said you'd leave without me if I wasn't," she reminded him.

"That was a joke." He took each of the women standing next to him by the arm. "Sidonie, I'd like you to meet Abby Hedgpeth. You know Cathy Sue. Abby, this is Sidonie Saddler."

Sidonie nodded at Cathy Sue, but her eyes were glued on Abby. She was holding on to Rafe's arm as if she'd never let go. "Pleased to meet you," Abby said shyly. She kept her eyes demurely downcast when she wasn't gazing adoringly at Rafe.

Sidonie wanted to scratch her eyes out, right after

she yanked her away from Rafe. Shocked by her sudden violent urges, she could only nod in response.

"Abby's the home economics teacher at the high school. This was her first year in Cache, and she did a marvelous job," gushed Cathy Sue, dropping Rafe's arm. "We're all hoping she'll decide to renew her contract for another year."

"Oh?" Sidonie said, instinctively aware of undercurrents. Cathy Sue and Abby were exchanging information, but she wasn't sure what they were saying to each other. "Cache is a nice town. Why would you want to leave?"

Cathy Sue answered for her. "There are so few suitable men. And Abby is eager to start her own family."

Abby blushed prettily, looking up at Rafe from under her eyelashes while keeping her death grip on his arm. It really was not necessary for her to cling to him that way. Sidonie started to cut into the line, next to Rafe, but Cathy Sue intercepted her, and Sidonie found herself neatly maneuvered into standing behind Rafe and Abby.

"But she's so young—she has plenty of time."

"Oh, I want to start as soon as possible," said Abby. "I want lots of children." She turned pink again when Rafe smiled at her.

"Some women are just born to be mothers, don't you think?" Cathy Sue asked archly.

She was looking at Sidonie, but the question was clearly meant for Rafe, so Sidonie didn't bother to answer. Now it was obvious what was going on. Cathy Sue was matchmaking. And from the way Rafe was looking at Abby—like he'd been poleaxed—Cathy Sue was on her way to succeeding. The image Sidonie had been carrying in her head changed abruptly. She faded from the picture. Rafe was still in the kitchen with the children, but now the boys and girls were all tiny blondes.

Sidonie wanted to cry. Which was crazy. She never cried. Not over a lost part, and never because of a man. She squared her shoulders. She wasn't about to start weeping now. But she had to get away, before she did something else to relieve her hurt feelings—like pour barbecue sauce over Abby's head. "This is taking a long time, Rafe. Maybe we should forget about lunch and hit the road."

"We're almost at the head of the line. It will only be a few more minutes."

Sidonie looked around. "We'll never find a table. Why don't you get our barbecue to go?"

"There's no need to rush away, Rafe," said Cathy Sue. "J.D. and Darcy are saving a table for us. But don't let us keep you, Sidonie."

"If he stays, I stay," Sidonie said through clenched teeth. "We came together."

"You and Rafe?" asked Abby. "Together?"

"Yes. We live together," said Sidonie, feeling mean and hateful.

Abby's eyes widened. "Oh, I didn't realize—" She dropped Rafe's arm, looking like a little girl who'd just had her lollipop taken away from her.

"Sidonie is Rafe's housekeeper," said Cathy Sue.

"That's not all I—"

"She's my landlord, too," Rafe interjected. "Sidonie owns the house I leased from her caretaker. She came home unexpectedly after she injured her knee, and found me on the premises. She needed a place to stay. I needed a housekeeper, so—"

"So you hired her. How kind of you." Abby took hold of his arm again and looked up at him adoringly.

"I don't know about that," said Rafe, avoiding Sidonie's disbelieving gaze.

She ought to kick his butt.

"We're all dying to see your new house. It won't be long until you'll be moving, will it?" asked Cathy Sue.

"Not long. Three or four more weeks."

"Will you be having a housewarming?" asked Abby.

"Sure thing. I've hired the caterer and I'm fattening up a steer to barbecue. Or I was, until Sidonie made a pet out of him."

"Goodness me. Two big social events within weeks. Cache may never be the same."

"Two?" asked Abby, innocently.

"The Spring Dance," said Cathy Sue. "You are going, aren't you, Rafe? We talked about it at lunch last week."

Rafe nodded. "I'll be there." He turned to Abby. "Will you be going?"

Her mouth drooped sadly. "No, I'm afraid not. I don't have an escort." She trained her baby blues on Rafe and said, "Unless…would you consider taking me?"

With only a momentary hesitation, Rafe said, "I'd be honored."

Sidonie sucked in her breath. A sharp pain in the vicinity of her heart left her speechless.

"Oh, thank you," Abby said, blushing. "I don't know what I'd have done if you'd said no. I've never asked a man out before."

Sidonie wanted to see a sly, triumphant gleam in

Abby's eyes, but all she saw was relief. Abby really had been afraid Rafe would turn her down.

"Good for you, Abby," said Cathy Sue, beaming. "I know that wasn't easy for an old-fashioned girl like you, but I'm sure Rafe must appreciate a few modern touches in a woman. This is the nineties, after all. Sidonie, isn't this nice?"

Sidonie blinked, swallowed and said testily, "Peachy."

"Well, I think it's wonderful," Cathy Sue cooed. "My two favorite people going to the dance together. Will you be attending, Sidonie?"

She managed a nonchalant shrug. "Maybe. If I'm still around."

"Are you planning on leaving soon?" asked Abby hopefully.

"As soon as my knee is better. I have an audition in Fort Worth next week."

"Audition? Are you an actress?"

"She's a chorus girl," said Cathy Sue, making it sound like Sidonie walked the streets.

An opinion Rafe had once shared, Sidonie recalled. She'd thought he'd changed his mind, but he wasn't leaping to her defense. How could she have thought he was anything but a pompous ass?

Simple. He'd been a different man the past two days, a man who knew how to have fun. Because he'd shown her that side of himself, she'd been on the verge of making a terrible mistake.

Lucky for her he'd reverted to type. Otherwise she might have fallen deeply and irrevocably in love with a man who thought she was less than perfect.

Numbly, Sidonie took the plate of ribs the counterman handed her. She followed Rafe, Cathy Sue and

Abby to a table in the corner. By the time she joined them, the only vacant seat was between Cathy Sue and Darcy. Abby was seated opposite Sidonie, between Rafe and J.D. At first J.D. didn't seem happy to see Rafe, but the two men talked more or less civilly about rotational grazing and the pluses and minuses of various breeds of cattle. Cathy Sue and Abby discussed recipes and shopping.

"Miss Sidonie?" Darcy asked softly.

"Yes, sweetie, what is it?"

"Would you...if you're going to be here a little longer...give me and Elizabeth a dance lesson?"

Sidonie swallowed and managed a weak smile. "Sure, kid. No problem."

"Cool! When?"

"When what?" asked Cathy Sue.

"Sidonie's going to give us dance lessons after all," crowed Darcy.

"Well. I thought you didn't want to teach dancing. What changed your mind?" asked Rafe.

"I haven't changed my mind. I'm not planning on teaching as a career. I'm going to give Darcy and Elizabeth one or two lessons."

"When?" repeated Darcy.

"How about Monday after school?"

"Great. I can't wait to tell Elizabeth. What should we wear? I've got a leotard and tights and ballet slippers, too. Mom got them for me for Christmas."

"That will be fine."

"Finish your lunch, Darcy," said Cathy Sue. "Remember all those starving children in Bosnia."

The adults returned to their conversations. Sidonie moved her food around on her plate and listened to the drone of voices. As the meal dragged on forever, her jaw began to ache from the effort of keeping a smile on her face. She wanted to yell at Rafe for forgetting what they'd shared the past two days. How could he be so eager to burn a bridge they'd only begun to cross?

Chapter Eight

Rafe whistled tunelessly as he drove out of San Antonio, headed north toward home. A man ought to whistle when he'd found what he'd been looking for. But he should also know better than to count chickens before they hatched. No question that Abby Hedgpeth had the look of the kind of woman he'd planned on marrying—demure, ladylike, serene. But looks could be deceiving. And he wasn't sure if he liked the way she'd asked him out. It was flattering, sure, but doing it in front of other people hadn't given him the option of saying no.

Rafe shook his head. There was no reason for him to be suspicious. Abby hadn't been trying to manipulate him into taking her to the dance. She'd probably needed other people around for moral support. She had said she'd never asked a man out before. Abby Hedgpeth was a real old-fashioned girl.

He glanced over at Sidonie. Thoroughly modern Sidonie, he would have called her a day or two ago.

But she liked old-fashioned kinds of fun—boat rides, rodeos, slow dancing. No doubt about it, he'd had a good time with Sidonie. But he couldn't spend all his time having fun. Having a good life required a man to be serious. He had to plan, set goals, work to achieve them. For that he needed a helpmate who knew how to be serious, too. Not a woman like Sidonie, all flash and fire.

Rafe looked at her again. Sidonie was jammed against the passenger door, as far from him as she could get. She didn't look happy. And she hadn't said a word since...when? She'd stopped talking around the time he'd agreed to take Abby to the Spring Dance.

He stopped whistling. That couldn't be what had her so uncharacteristically quiet. Sidonie couldn't have thought he was going to ask her to the dance. He'd made it clear from the beginning that she was not his type. Besides, if she'd wanted to go to the dance with him, she would have asked him—and she wouldn't have been shy about it, either. Something was bothering her, though.

"Do you feel all right?"

"Fine."

"Are you sure? You didn't eat much lunch."

"I wasn't hungry."

She continued to stare out the window, refusing to even look at him.

Clearing his throat, he tried again. "What did you think of the livestock show? Did you find any business you'd like to go into?"

"No."

"Nothing? Not even llamas or potbellied pigs?"

"No."

"That's probably a wise decision. True, they aren't

slaughtered, but you'd have to sell a lot of them to make a living. I don't think the demand is there. But there are other options. For instance, how about a goat dairy? Goat cheese and milk are gourmet items—it wouldn't take a large herd to be profitable."

"I don't want to raise goats for milk, or sheep for wool, or pigs for pets!" Her voice shook. "I want to dance. And I want to travel. I hate staying in one place very long."

"You don't say?" He'd been wrong. The fun they'd shared the past two days hadn't impressed her at all. He should have known—Sidonie had a lot of her mother in her. "So when are you leaving? Soon?"

"Not soon enough," she said in a voice that would freeze fire.

Rafe gripped the steering wheel until his knuckles whitened. "You really think you're going to dance again, don't you?"

"I *am* going to dance again."

"What if you're wrong?"

She shrugged. "I'll worry about that when the time comes."

"That's a real mature attitude. When are you going to grow up?"

"I am grown-up. Too grown-up for someone like you, obviously. Get 'em young and train 'em right, is that the plan?"

"What are you talking about?"

Sidonie slanted him a look that would scorch steel.

"I'm talking about What's-her-name Hedgehog. The girl you were drooling over at lunch."

"Abby Hedgpeth is her name," he said through clenched teeth. Okay, so maybe he shouldn't have accepted an invitation from one woman when he was still—technically—escorting another. But there was no need for Sidonie to blame a sweet woman like Abby for his behavior.

Sidonie had been around the block. She ought to be able to recognize a harmless flirtation when she saw it. He sure as hell hadn't given her any reason to expect anything more than a few kisses from him. "And I was not drooling over her."

"No? My mistake. That wet on your chin must have been because of Cathy Sue then. You're still in love with her."

"I was never in love with Cathy Sue! If my chin was wet, you're the reason. You'd make a saint mad enough to spit."

"Well, Saint McMasters, if you never loved Cathy Sue, why are you looking for her clone?"

"I'm looking for a woman to share my life with, someone who likes the same things I like, someone who'll be a good rancher's wife. You got a problem with that?"

"Yes. What about love?"

"What about it?"

"Don't you want it?"

"Not particularly. If there is such a thing, I expect it will grow in time—from similar backgrounds and mutual interests."

"Stuffy's back, and Hedgehog's got him," sneered Sidonie, crossing her arms across her chest.

"Stop calling her Hedgehog. What's the matter with you? Abby didn't do anything to you."

"She sure did something to you."

"She asked me to the Spring Dance. That's all."

"And you couldn't wait to say yes."

"I didn't have any reason to say no."

"Didn't you? Don't you think she's a little young for you? You know, Rafe, you may be confusing youth and innocence with perfection. The hedgehog—excuse me, Miss Hedgpeth—may look perfect only because she hasn't been around long enough to make any mistakes, much less learn from them."

"Stuff it, Sidonie. I'm not discussing Abby with you."

"She's the one, isn't she? The girl with your six essential requirements."

Rafe's eyebrows shot up. "What do you know about my essentials?"

"Everything. You want a woman who is country born and bred, and a good homemaker. Someone who's maternal, respectable, attractive and—gag me with a spoon—docile."

"You said you would stay out of my study."

"No, I didn't. You told me to stay out, but I never agreed. It is my house, after all."

"That doesn't give you the right to poke your nose in my journal. My plans are my business."

"And your plan is finally complete. You've found Miss Perfect."

"Listen up, woman! Just because you never made a plan in your life—"

"And I never will. Plans are so pedestrian. I *like* not knowing what's going to happen next."

"If that's your attitude, there's no point in trying to reason with you."

"There's no point in making plans. There are too many things that can go wrong. I could get run over by a truck tomorrow. I'll just take my chances that something will turn up when I need it. It's worked for me so far."

"Sidonie—" He'd been about to suggest she think about her future again. She wouldn't, no matter what he said. And he wasn't going to do it for her, not again. She didn't want to teach, and she didn't want to ranch. Fine. She'd gotten this far without a plan, maybe she'd continue to be lucky. Once her dancing career was finished, she'd probably find some man to take care of her. Heaven help the poor sucker, whoever he was.

"Well? What were you about to say?"

"Nothing. Do whatever you want to do. It's your life."

She stuck her nose in the air in that infuriating way she had. "About time you figured that out."

"What about you? You wouldn't be so bent out of shape over Abby if you weren't trying to run my life."

"Excuse me? I'm not the one who arranged for you to meet your idea of the perfect woman. Blame Cathy Sue for that."

"Cathy Sue was only trying to help me out."

"Really? What's in it for her?"

"Not a damn thing. She's a friend, that's all."

"Did you ever think this might be her revenge? Maybe Abby isn't what she appears to be."

"Helping out is what country people do for one another. And they do it with no strings attached."

"That may be, but I for one have had enough of the country. I can't wait to go to Fort Worth." She sat back, crossed her arms over her chest and stared out the window.

The audition. Damn. The first real-life test of her injured knee, and he'd forgotten all about it. He wanted to tell her he was sorry. For what, he wasn't sure, but he figured she'd never let him know what she was feeling as long as she was mad at him. Poor kid. She was probably scared out of her wits. He couldn't imagine how bad she'd feel when she didn't get the job. And she wouldn't. Or if she, by some miracle, made it through the tryout, she wouldn't last. Her knee was better—she didn't limp any longer and she hadn't worn her brace in days—but it would never stand the strain of eight shows a week.

"There's a Dairy Queen. Want to stop for a dipped cone?"

She gave him a suspicious look. "No, but I'd go for a hot-fudge sundae. If you apologize first."

He might want to say he was sorry, but damned if he'd do it on command. "Apologize? What for?"

"If you don't know—"

"Sidonie, I'm sorry," he said quickly. "For anything and everything I've ever done. Do you want to stop at the DQ or not?"

"Yes."

When they were seated in a booth eating their ice cream, Sidonie surprised him again.

Licking a drop of fudge sauce off her upper lip, she looked at him, then lowered her eyes. "I'm sorry, too," she mumbled.

"What was that?"

Her chin came up, and she glared at him. "I said I'm sorry, too."

Rafe took a bite of his cone. "Apology accepted. Do you know what you're sorry for?"

"For making all those cracks about Abby. She seems like a very nice girl—woman."

"Yes. She does."

"She has a lot of good qualities."

"Looks that way."

"But, then, so do I."

"True. Different qualities, but still good."

She nodded. "So you surely didn't think I was jealous, did you?"

"The thought crossed my mind," he admitted, probably unwisely.

Sure enough, Sidonie's eyes began shooting sparks and her stubborn little chin jutted out. "Believe me, Rafe. I wasn't any more jealous of Abby than you were of that waiter I danced with."

Didn't she know a man would be a fool to get jealous over a woman who couldn't wait to leave town? Through clenched teeth, Rafe said, "Didn't I hear you tell Darcy you're going to Fort Worth Tuesday?"

"Yes."

"But you'll be back?"

"For a few weeks. The musicals at Casa Mañana won't start rehearsals right away."

"You seem pretty confident you'll get the job."

"I'm very good at what I do. And in some circles I actually have a reputation for being competent and reliable."

"I can believe that." He wanted to tell her more— that if she didn't get the job, she'd still have a place to come home to, where she had friends who'd help her do whatever she needed to do to get on with her life. But he wouldn't bring up any doubts about her ability to continue dancing, not again. He'd done everything he could to remind her she had another heritage, the one her father had left her. It hadn't been enough. All he could do now was wish her well. "Good luck, Sidonie."

Monday afternoon, Sidonie stood at the front window, watching for Maggie and the girls. As usual, her foolish mind took the opportunity to rerun her last conversation with Rafe, starting with dairy goats and ending with a halfhearted "good luck."

She didn't need luck. Belle had always said luck was nothing more than opportunity meeting preparation. She hadn't been prepared for Rafe McMasters. And she hadn't been looking for the opportunity to fall in love with a stuffed shirt who liked his women respectable and docile.

Some opportunity that was.

Corny said never pass one up. Well, she'd add her own twist to that motto—*always* pass up the opportunity to have your heart stomped on. Too bad she hadn't learned that lesson sooner, before her own silly heart had tripped and fallen for a certain sexy cowboy masquerading as a somber businessman.

Sidonie needed to get away from Cache. Ever since they had returned from San Antonio, her home had seemed more like a cage than a sanctuary. If she knew what was good for her, she'd pack up her pickup and head for Fort Worth today. With a little bit of luck, once she was away from Rafe, she would fall out of love just as fast as she'd fallen in. Only problem was, lately her luck had been all bad. She sighed a long shuddering sigh as tears slid down her cheeks.

Sidonie immediately scrubbed the offending moisture from her face. She was not going to cry over Rafe! She be darned if she would let herself wallow in misery and self-pity over that stubborn, self-righteous—

Rafe chose that moment to come out of his study. "Someone's coming up the drive."

Taking a deep breath, she managed a civil nod in

his direction. "It's Maggie. She's bringing Elizabeth and Darcy for the lesson I promised them."

He went to the front door and opened it. "That's not Maggie."

Sidonie joined him in the doorway. "No, it's not. Abby Hedgpeth. Isn't that a nice surprise for you?"

"Sidonie, don't start," he warned, heading out the door to greet their visitors.

While Rafe opened the driver-side door and helped Abby out of the car, the two young girls exploded out of the passenger door, each carrying a small bag. "Hi, Sidonie!" squealed Elizabeth, racing up the steps to the front porch. "This is my friend, Darcy."

"We've met. Hello, Darcy. It's nice to see you again. Do you both have your leotards and tights?"

"Yes, ma'am," said Darcy. "Where can we change?"

"You can use my room. Elizabeth, you know where it is, don't you?"

"Sure."

When she looked around, Abby and Rafe had disappeared from the hall. She heard their voices coming from the parlor.

"Cathy Sue was busy, so I said I'd bring the girls for their lesson."

"Is Maggie picking them up?" asked Rafe.

"Well, no. I was going to wait for them. That's all right, isn't it?"

"Of course," said Rafe. "I was just going up to my house. The contractor is meeting me for a final inspection. Would you like to join me?"

"I'd love to. I'll be the envy of the whole town. Everyone's dying to see your house." Abby took Rafe by the arm. She looked over her shoulder at Sidonie as they walked away. "How long will the lesson last?"

Sidonie glanced at the hall clock. "An hour, at least. But don't hurry back. Take as much time as you need." She wanted to tell Rafe if he wasn't back in thirty minutes, she was coming after him, but she didn't. If he thought Abby was the woman for him, then she couldn't compete—not if he was still fixated on his dumb essentials.

"Miss Sidonie? We're ready."

After the lesson was over, the trio went back to the house. While the girls were changing back into their jeans and sweaters, Sidonie rejoined Gypsy at the front window. It had been over an hour since Rafe and Abby had walked up the hill together. How long could it take to look at a house, even a large house?

"They must be having a good time up there," she told Gypsy, turning away from the window.

The dog wagged her short tail and barked. Sidonie looked again. Rafe and Abby were strolling down the hill arm in arm. She was still clinging to him as they entered the foyer.

Sidonie forced a smile. "Hi. How was the tour?"

"Wonderful!" gushed Abby. "The house is beautiful, don't you agree?"

"I wouldn't know," said Sidonie. "I haven't seen it."

"No?" Abby looked up at Rafe, her cheeks pink. "Then I was your first guest?"

"You could say that. If you don't count the decorator and her crew."

"I am honored, sir." She gave him a perky grin.

Sidonie ground her teeth together. She might have

known Abby would be perky, when she got over being shy. "The girls should be almost ready to go."

"How was the lesson?"

"It went very well." Once she'd stopped torturing herself imagining what Rafe and Abby were doing, she'd actually enjoyed Darcy and Elizabeth's lesson. They'd made up in enthusiasm what they'd lacked in experience.

The two budding ballerinas came down the hall. "Thanks, Sidonie. The lesson was great!" said Elizabeth.

"Fantastic!" agreed Darcy. "Can we do this again?"

"Sure. As long as I'm around. I'll call your mothers when I get back from Fort Worth, and we'll set up another lesson."

Both girls hugged her, then followed Abby to the car. As they drove off, waving, Sidonie turned to Rafe. "Well, it looks like your plan is coming along nicely. Your house is almost finished, and you've found a prime candidate for Mrs. McMasters. It was nice of Cathy Sue to arrange for you and Abby to meet. Why do you suppose she did that?"

"She probably didn't trust me to do the job right."

"She should have. You two seem to value the same essentials."

"Would you stop harping on my essentials?"

"Okay. I'm sorry. But I still think choosing a wife the same way you choose a cow is a mistake."

"How would you do it?"

"I'd wait until I fell in love."

"I thought so. As usual, no plan for Sidonie."

"Did you plan to fall in love with Cathy Sue?"

"I never was in love with Cathy Sue."

"Oh, no? Then why did you ask her to marry you? You didn't have your list prepared back then, did you?"

"I had a plan, the same one I have today. But I hadn't refined it or written it down. If I had thought things through, I would have known sooner that Cathy Sue and I wanted different things. But I was young and impatient, and I made a foolish mistake."

"How did that happen?"

"Cathy Sue more or less maneuvered me into proposing when I did."

"I noticed she's good at maneuvering."

"Yeah. I'd planned to wait until I got my own place before I thought about settling down. But Cathy Sue decided we should get married sooner than that, and it seemed like a good idea at the time. But her real agenda got clearer once I had my accident. She was happy about that."

"Happy you were hurt?"

"Happy I'd lost my livelihood. She assumed I'd have to knuckle under and work for Emmet—something she'd been after me to do from the beginning. She knew I wanted my own spread, but she'd have lost her position as Queen of Proffit County if she'd left her father's home to help me build up my ranch. I couldn't have matched the Clancy place for years."

"So she wanted you to live with her and her father?"

"Right. She hinted that if I did, I'd inherit the Clancy ranch someday, but I knew that wasn't likely. Anyway, I didn't want to spend my life working for a man and waiting for him to die. I wanted my own place. And Cathy Sue wasn't willing to wait until I got it."

"Having your own land is important to you."

"I'll be the first McMasters in Proffit County to own my own place. I want to build on that, have something to leave my sons."

"And daughters?"

"And daughters. There are six bedrooms in my house, besides the master suite. Plenty of room for both sons and daughters."

"Six?" Sidonie said faintly. "You do need a young wife. Abby is perfect."

The following Friday Sidonie unpacked her suitcase as Maggie sat on her bed and watched.

"So how did the audition go?" asked Maggie.

"Fine."

"No problem with the knee?"

"Not even a twinge. I got the job, if I want it."

"Great! I think. You don't seem too happy about it."

"For some reason the reality of dancing again didn't match up to the anticipation."

"Hmm. I wonder why not?"

Shrugging, Sidonie took the new dress she'd bought out of the suitcase and reached for a hanger. "I don't know. Maybe I forgot about the downside of a dancing career—the endless rehearsals, living out of a suitcase, always eating in restaurants or hotel rooms."

"I thought those were the things you enjoyed."

"Yeah. Me, too." Sidonie sighed and turned back to the closet.

"Wait a minute. Show me that dress."

Sidonie held the dress in front of her. "I got it at Neiman-Marcus—on sale—to wear to the Spring Dance."

"Try it on. I want to see how it looks on you."

Sidonie took off her royal blue jumpsuit. She slipped the dress over her head and let it slide over her body.

"Wow! Where's the rest of it?" Maggie walked slowly around Sidonie, her mouth hanging open.

Sidonie glanced in the mirror. The hot pink slip dress covered all the important parts. Barely. "This is it. Too much?"

"Not nearly enough. You can't wear that to the Spring Dance, not unless you want to start a riot."

"A riot might be nice," Sidonie said absently. Except for a few moments onstage at Casa Mañana, life had been dull, dull, dull ever since San Antonio. Dull activities: cooking, cleaning, exercises. Dull conversation: "I'm going to town" or "I'll be in my study."

And a dull ache in her heart. Stupid heart. Jumping off a cliff into love with a man who wanted Miss Perfect.

"I'm serious, Sidonie. Don't you have something else to wear?"

She shrugged, and one of the narrow straps slid off her shoulder. "What difference does it make?"

"What's wrong with you? You're not your usual perky self."

"Perky? I've never been perky in my life." Abigail Hedgpeth was perky. When she wasn't being sweet and innocent and perfect.

"All right, wrong word. Why aren't you your usual saucy, scintillating self?"

Flopping onto the bed, Sidonie stared at the ceiling. "I don't have a single 'scintil' left in me."

"Oh, no! It's your knee, isn't it? You're afraid it

won't hold up once rehearsals start. But Rayburn said it was much better, almost a hundred percent again."

"It is a hundred percent better. And I'm sure it will hold up."

"Then why—" Maggie's eyes rounded. "Oh."

Sidonie raised herself on her elbows. "'Oh'? What does that mean?"

"Nothing. I was wrong about the dress. It's perfect."

Groaning, Sidonie sat up. "Nothing about me is perfect. That's the problem."

"I thought so. It's Rafe, isn't it?"

"Rafe? Don't be silly. He doesn't have anything to do with...anything."

"Sidonie?" Maggie sat down next to her on the edge of the bed. "Are you in love with him?"

Sidonie shook her head fiercely. "No!" When tears filled her eyes, she hung her head and nodded. "Yes," she whispered miserably. "I don't want to be. I didn't mean to be. How did it happen, Maggie? A person's heart ought to know better than to fall for a sanctimonious stuffed shirt." Except now she knew that Rafe's shirt was stuffed with a rowdy, hell-raising cowboy.

"Oh, my. Poor Sidonie. Are you sure you want to go to the dance?"

Her chin came up. "I'm not a coward."

"Of course not. But Rafe will be there with Abby. Seeing them together—won't that hurt?"

"Yes, but once I see him making a fool of himself over her, I'll fall out of love." She looked hopefully at Maggie. "Won't I? I'm planning on it."

"I guess that's possible," said Maggie. She didn't

sound convinced. "And that dress is to let him know what he's missing?"

"Something like that."

"Do you need a date? You might feel more confident if you didn't have to go alone. Cache is kind of short on bachelors these days, but Rayburn must know someone."

"No." Sidonie would have liked to argue with Maggie about her confidence level, but she didn't have the energy. Or the conviction. "Judge Longstreet is escorting me. I had to ask him, of course, but he agreed to take me."

"You'd better wear a coat. The judge will have apoplexy if he sees you in that dress."

"I've got a shawl—red and pink poppies on a black ground, with gold fringe. I'll wear it until we get to the country club. After that, watch out! I'll show Mr. Rafe McMasters a few essentials he never planned on."

Chapter Nine

Saturday evening Sidonie draped the colorful shawl around her shoulders and paced the parlor floor. Gypsy and Jasmine paced with her, while Magnolia and Zorro stalked the trio, leaping out at them from beneath the sofa or from behind the lace curtains. She'd gotten ready too soon, although she wasn't sure why. She was not eager for the evening to begin.

"On the other hand, the sooner it starts the sooner it will be over," she told her furry audience.

She hadn't seen Rafe since noon. She'd spent the afternoon hiding in her studio, working herself hard, trying not to think about Rafe getting ready for his big date. She hadn't succeeded, but at least she hadn't actually seen him in his best suit, whistling a happy tune. He'd whistled a lot lately—he was so pleased with himself and the success of his plans, he made her sick.

Sidonie hadn't come in the house until she'd heard him drive off at six o'clock. The dance didn't begin until eight, but Abby had invited him to her house for dinner. She could imagine what kind of meal a home economics teacher would prepare—nothing burnt or lumpy or badly seasoned. No, the hedgehog would serve Rafe a perfect meal, the start of a perfect evening. For them.

A tear seeped out from beneath her lashes and rolled down her cheek. Angrily, Sidonie dashed it away. If Rafe didn't want her, she'd learn to live with it. He never would have done more than "want" anyway. If Abby hadn't come along, Rafe might have lowered his standards enough to indulge in a spring fling with her. But she wouldn't have settled for that—no matter what Rafe McMasters thought about chorus girls, she was not the flinging kind. Snapping her fingers, Sidonie clicked her heels in an impromptu flamenco dance. Her stomping sent Gypsy and the cats flying for cover.

There was a knock on the door, and she opened it.

"Good evening, Sidonie," said Judge Longstreet. "My, don't you look like a picture."

"Thank you, Judge." She curtsied.

"And ready right on time, too. Shall we go?" The judge extended his arm and led Sidonie to his immaculate 1967 Cadillac.

The short drive to the country club didn't give Sidonie enough time to compose herself. When they walked through the door, her heart was beating wildly and her palms were sweaty. "Only stage fright," she muttered. She'd gotten through worse, she was sure.

Only she couldn't remember what or when.

They entered what was usually the country club's dining room. It had been transformed into a spring bower by wooden trellises covered with silk and paper flowers. The tables had been moved to the edge of the room, leaving a large area open for dancing. Sidonie couldn't keep from searching the crowd for Rafe, but she didn't see him.

"Sidonie! Judge Longstreet! Over here!"

"Mrs. Dr. Parker is calling us," said the judge, steering Sidonie to the table where Maggie and Rayburn were sitting.

After they were seated and the judge and Rayburn were engaged in conversation, Maggie whispered to Sidonie, "They're not here yet. But it's early, only a few minutes after eight."

"They're probably lingering over dessert," said Sidonie, wishing she didn't have such a vivid imagination. She could see Abby feeding bites of something rich and chocolate to Rafe, letting her fingertips linger on his lips. Sidonie groaned.

"Are you okay?" Maggie asked.

"No. I think I'm going to be sick." Her hand fluttered over her churning stomach.

"Oh, no! Do you want Rayburn to give you something? His medical bag is in the car."

"No, no. I'll be all right." As soon as she saw Rafe and Abby together and got used to the idea that, unlike musical comedy, life didn't always have a happy ending. "Judge, would you care to dance?"

"My pleasure."

His eyes almost popped out of his head as Sidonie stood and dropped the shawl she'd been clutching around her shoulders. "Oh, my." He harrumphed once, but recovered quickly, taking her in his arms and whirling her onto the dance floor.

Sidonie's stomach settled down after a few turns around the dimly lighted room, and she'd almost relaxed when she saw them. Rafe, tall and handsome in his tailored dark blue suit, was shepherding Abby to a secluded table across the dance floor from the spot Maggie and Rayburn had chosen. Abby looked radiant, her petite frame tastefully covered in beige taffeta and lace.

Sidonie stumbled and stepped on the judge's toe. "Oh, sorry," she murmured.

"My fault, I'm sure," said the judge. "I don't get many opportunities to dance with a beautiful young woman."

"It was my fault," she assured him. She should have been prepared, but the shock of actually seeing Rafe with his arm around Abby's slender waist had made her clumsy. "You're a wonderful dancer."

The judge executed a complicated step with a flourish. "Belle gave me a few lessons. At a Spring Dance twenty-five years ago."

"Did she?" Something about the way he wouldn't meet her gaze caught her attention, giving her a welcome reason to block Rafe and Abby from her thoughts. She focused on the judge. "Tyler Longstreet, did you have a crush on my mother?"

He managed to look scandalized and guilty at the same time. "She was a married woman."

"She's a widow now."

"She's a career woman."

"She's a lonely woman." Sidonie hadn't realized the words were true until she spoke them out loud. Her mother was lonely and something else—a sudden insight told her Belle was tired of always being on the move. "Sometimes she misses the life she left behind when she returned to the stage."

"Small-town life? Belle?"

"I think so. Although she might not remember..." Everything small towns have to offer. Sidonie caught a glimpse of Rafe as he danced by with Abby snuggled tight in his arms. She looked away, ignoring the pinched feeling in her chest. Sidonie directed a brilliant smile at the judge. "Why don't you visit her? She'll be in London for another two months, at least."

"She wouldn't want to see me. She must have scores of sophisticated, worldly friends."

"Not really. She doesn't stay in one place long enough to make friends. Besides, old friends are the best, don't you think?"

"I've always wanted to go to England," mused the judge. "Lots of legal history there—the Old Bailey, the Houses of Parliament, the Inns of Court."

"She could show you all that and more." And he might remind Belle of a few things she'd forgotten about—roots and family and home.

Sidonie realized suddenly that she'd always wanted those things, even though for years her longing had stayed buried deep in her psyche. On some level she'd always wanted the life her mother had abandoned, and no wonder. She was her father's daughter, as well as her mother's. And even a rolling stone like her mother had to stop sometime. When she'd met Buck Saddler, it had been the wrong time, but now—with a little nudge from the judge—Belle might finally be ready to gather some moss.

"I haven't had a real vacation in years. I'll do it!"

"Good for you. We'll call Mother tomorrow and let her make the arrangements. After all her years on the road, she's better than a travel agent."

"Hey, Judge, old buddy, how about letting me cut in?" A young man snatched Sidonie out of the judge's arms before either of them had time to react.

"Hello, darlin'," he said, as he wrapped his arms

around her and pulled her much too close. "I've been waiting for someone like you for a long, long time."

"My, isn't the music nice?" said Abby, looking wistfully at Rafe. Abby had her wistful look down pat, Rafe had discovered. Not to mention her shy look, her doubtful look and her adoring look. Rafe winced. He shouldn't make fun of her. Abby was a nice woman, a woman who'd make a man a good wife. She had all the essentials.

And she bored him senseless.

"Would you like to dance?" When she nodded shyly, Rafe got up and led her onto the floor.

"Oh, look," said Abby, peeking around his shoulder. "There's your housekeeper."

Rafe jerked his head in the direction she'd indicated.

"My, isn't that dress...daring? I'd never have the nerve to wear something like that." Abby batted her eyelashes at him and turned pink.

Abby blushed easily and often, he'd discovered. And she didn't miss an opportunity to talk about Sidonie. Abby was more than a little curious about his relationship with his "housekeeper." But Abby was much too polite to ask flat out what was going on between the two of them. Not that he could have answered her if she'd been so bold. He didn't have a clue.

Rafe sneaked a look at his watch, knowing that the night had just begun. It would be hours before he could reasonably take Abby home.

And leave her there. She was not the woman for him.

Rafe stared at Sidonie, frowning. She was dancing much too close to her partner, and she was smiling.

She hadn't smiled at him in days. She hadn't smiled at all since she'd returned from Fort Worth. She hadn't said so, but he knew she hadn't gotten the job. He'd been waiting for her to tell him, so he could do something, anything, to put the sparkle back in her blue eyes. And now here she was, sparkling all over some other guy.

The man—boy, really—she was dancing with swung her away, then pulled her back. When she twirled into his arms, her skirt, already too short in his opinion, flared high enough to give everyone in the room a good look at her impossibly long legs. "Who's that dancing with Sidonie?"

"Bobby Lee Hudson," Abby said, sniffing. "He's the assistant coach. He's leaving Cache at the end of the school year."

Not soon enough, thought Rafe. "You sound as if you'll be glad to see him go."

"I'm sure I don't care one way or the other. Coach Hudson doesn't mean anything to me."

"He doesn't?"

"Oh, we dated a few times. But I was too tame for him. He told me he likes his women worldly. Would you say Sidonie is that kind of woman? Experienced?"

"She's not tame. That's for sure," Rafe muttered.

"I didn't think so." Abby gasped. "Look at that— he's taking her out on the patio. The nerve—right in front of the whole town."

"Maybe they want some fresh air. It is a little warm in here, don't you think?"

"Why is he taking her outside?" wailed Abby. "He just met her. He's not even her date, for heaven's sake."

Rafe stared at Abby. She was more animated than she'd been all evening. And he had a feeling it wasn't because of him. "Abby, would you like to go outside?"

"I sure would."

She raced for the door, and Rafe followed. It was dark outside, and it took a few minutes for his eyes to adjust. The patio and the benches that edged it were empty. A brick walkway led through the oleander bushes bordering the patio to the pool. Rafe started down the path after Abby, not sure what they were doing, or why.

"That's enough, Bobby Lee. Stop it!"

"Aw, come on, babe. Just one little kiss."

Rafe lengthened his stride, almost running the last few yards to the pool. As he rounded the last bush, he took in the scene by the pool house. Abby was staring wide-eyed at Bobby Lee and Sidonie. The coach had one arm around Sidonie's waist, the other on her nape. He was forcing her head closer to his and she was trying, unsuccessfully, to push him away. "Let her go!" Rafe ordered.

Bobby Lee glanced in his direction, but focused on Abby, who was standing slightly behind him. "I don't think so. She's hot for me."

"In your dreams, buster!" said Sidonie, aiming a kick at his shins. She missed and, losing her balance, fell against Bobby Lee.

He tightened his hold on her, shoving her face into his chest, muffling Sidonie's indignant squeals. "See what I mean? She's all over me."

"Take your hands off her," warned Rafe.

"Bobby Lee Hudson! Do what the man says!" Abby said.

"Oww! She bit me!" Bobby Lee released Sidonie and rubbed his chest. She staggered back a step before Bobby Lee recovered and snagged her wrist. "Like to play rough, huh? That's okay with me. Come here, darlin'." He jerked her back into his arms.

Rafe tapped him on the shoulder. "Maybe you didn't hear me. I said, let her go."

"I heard you. You listen to me. Stay out of this. This is between me and her."

"Not anymore." Rafe spun him around, drew back a fist and socked Bobby Lee on the chin, snapping his head back.

Bobby Lee shook his head, as if to clear it. Then he straightened up and slowly shrugged out of his jacket. "Wanna fight, huh?" He glanced at Sidonie, a sly grin twisting his mouth. "She must be hot stuff, if you're still willing to fight over her. You two have been living together for weeks, right? I'd have thought you'd have gotten all she had to give by now—and you did bring another woman to the dance." Bobby Lee narrowed his eyes and looked straight at Abby Hedgpeth, then threw his jacket onto a pool chair and raised his fists in a classic boxer's pose.

Rafe took off his suit coat and loosened his tie.

"Hold this," he said, handing his coat to Sidonie.

She let it fall to the ground. "Stop it, both of you! You're acting like…men!"

Rafe ignored her and he and Bobby Lee began circling one another.

"Fight!" someone shouted, and the poolside was suddenly filled with spectators.

Abby was standing in the front row, not far from Sidonie. Rafe registered her shocked expression a second before Bobby Lee landed a blow to his midsection. It was the only time the younger man hit him. Rafe grunted, then hit the kid on the jaw with his right fist, following up with a left uppercut to the chin. Bobby Lee's eyes glazed over and he fell backward into the pool.

Several people applauded. Sidonie stood, hands on hips, tapping her toe and glaring at him. Abby was next to her. Rafe took a step toward her. "Abby, I—"

She backed away from him, hands outstretched in front of her. "Don't come near me, you...you brute!" She turned and pushed her way through the crowd to the pool. Kneeling, she held out her hand and helped the coach out of the water. "Bobby Lee, honeykins, are you all right?"

Rafe stared at his date. Obviously she hadn't found him any more interesting than he'd found her. He ought to tell her good-night, at least, but Abby didn't look like she had anything to say to him.

Sidonie, however, looked as if she'd bust if she didn't get a chance to tell him a few things. He leaned down and snagged his suit coat off the ground, then took her by the arm. "Looks like I'm stuck with you. Let's go."

"Are you nuts?" She tried jerking her arm free, but he held on. "What makes you think I'd go anywhere with you?"

"I won the fight. You're the prize."

Someone in the crowd gasped. Rafe put his hand on the small of Sidonie's back and pushed her through the throng of spectators.

"Stop shoving me, Rafe McMasters."

"Then walk faster, Sidonie Saddler. We're getting out of here."

"I guess we do have to leave, since you managed to ruin my evening."

"Me ruin *your* evening?" He was flabbergasted. Stopping, he turned her around so she was facing him. "You enjoy being mauled?"

"No." Her chin came up and she glared at him in that snooty way she had—like she was Queen of Everything and he was a lowly peasant. "But I could have handled the situation."

"The 'situation' was out of hand."

"It was not!"

"Oh, yes it was. And you brought it on yourself, dressing like a...chorus girl."

Sidonie poked him in the chest with her forefinger. "Let's get one thing straight, Mr. McMasters. Dancing in the chorus is what I do, not what I am."

He grabbed her shoulders, turned her around and kept her moving in front of him. "What's that supposed to mean?" he snarled in her ear.

"It means I am not a bimbo. I'm a lady, even by your antiquated standards."

"I never saw a lady wear a dress like that. No wonder that poor guy thought you were hot for him."

She gave an outraged gasp. "If that's what you think, I'm definitely not going anywhere with you," she said, digging in her heels and shoving back against him.

"Yes, you are." He picked her up and tossed her over his shoulder.

"I can't go with you," she yelled, beating on his back with her fists. "I came with Judge Longstreet. A lady always goes home with the man who brought her."

The judge was standing on the patio, just outside

the door. He held the door open as Rafe swept through.

"Evening, Judge." Rafe nodded as they passed him by. "I'm taking Sidonie home, if you don't have any objection."

"None at all. That's all right. That's fine. As a matter of fact, you'll be doing me a favor. I'm not ready to leave yet."

"Judge! He's kidnapping me! Do something!"

"I'll call you tomorrow," the judge said. "Have a nice evening." He waved goodbye.

"Here's your shawl," said Maggie, running after them. She handed it to Sidonie as Rafe carried her out the front door of the country club and into the parking lot. "Don't worry about Abby, Rafe. Bobby Lee is taking her home, as soon as he dries off."

Rafe opened the door to his car and stuffed her into the passenger seat. "Stay."

Wonder of wonders, she stayed. When he slid into the driver's side, Sidonie was sitting with her arms crossed in front of her chest and her nose in the air.

He started the engine and shifted into Drive. Sidonie kept her lips tightly pursed. He smiled. That wouldn't last. She might think she'd show her disapproval with the silent treatment, but he knew better. She couldn't keep her mouth shut for long. Nope. A man would always know where he stood with Sidonie. If he was too dumb to figure it out for himself, she'd tell him. Loudly and often.

Rafe laughed.

"What are you laughing about?"

"Nothing in particular. I feel good."

"You feel good? After what you did? Knocking that poor boy into the pool, carrying me out of the country club on your shoulder! What got into you? I thought you didn't like being talked about.''

"I don't.''

"Then why did you—''

Rafe peeled out of the parking lot, sending gravel flying. His good humor was fading fast. "I don't know.''

He took a corner on two wheels, sending Sidonie sliding against him. She tried to move away, but he wrapped his arm around her shoulders and fitted her against his side. Driving with one hand, he played with the strap of her dress with the other.

"What are you doing?'' She batted ineffectually at his hand.

"I don't know,'' he repeated. He slid his fingers along the neckline—the very low neckline—of her dress. "I'm being spontaneous.''

"That's not like you.'' She sounded a little breathless. Now she was holding his hand against the slope of her breast.

"No, it's not. Neither is brawling over a woman, but no one in Cache will ever believe that.''

"You'll be the talk of the town again.''

"True enough. And it's all your fault.''

"My fault!'' She pushed his hand away.

"You wore that dress. You danced with another man. You made me crazy.''

"I did?''

The redheaded hussy batted her eyes at him. She was trying to make him nuts. She deserved whatever she got. "And you're going to pay.''

"I am?''

"Oh, yeah. Big-time.''

He turned off the road onto a narrow lane.

"Where are we going? This isn't the way home."
She sounded a little nervous. He didn't care.

"Yes, it is. A shortcut."

"I don't want to go home. It's too early."

"No, you're wrong. It's too late."

"Too late for what? Never mind. I don't see why
we couldn't have stayed at the country club until the
dance was over."

"Because. I don't belong there. And neither do you,
honey." He raked his gaze over her, taking in her
tousled red hair, her sexy dress with the strap slipping
off her shoulder. Why did she have to make every
other woman pale in comparison? She was making
him want like he'd never wanted before.

Suddenly everything about her irritated the hell out
of him. "You may not be a bimbo, but you're no
lady."

Something flared in her eyes, something that might
have been pain. Oh, hell, he'd hurt her feelings. He
pulled up in front of Buck's house and reached for
her, but the hurt look was gone in a flash, replaced by
obvious anger.

"You're no gentleman, either!" she railed. "A gentleman wouldn't leave his date stranded." She opened
the car door, got out and raced to the front door.

Rafe got out of the car and walked slowly after her.
There was no reason to hurry, as far as he could see.
He'd make sure they had all the time they needed.
"Abby wasn't stranded. She had Bobby Lee, remem-
ber? Abby didn't want to be with me any more than
I wanted to be with her. She wants a gentleman. I
wasn't one fifteen years ago, and I'm not one now."

"Neither is Bobby Lee." Sidonie had reached the

top step leading to the front porch and turned to face him.

"Not now, but he's young. She probably thinks she can change him."

"Like Cathy Sue tried to change you?"

"It didn't work then, and I'm too old now. I guess I'll never be a gentleman."

"And you think no *lady* is going to take you as you are, is that it?"

Rafe nodded. "But you will, won't you?"

Something in his eyes must have startled her. She spun around and ran the few steps to the front door. He caught up with her as she reached the door. Before she could open it, Rafe grabbed her by the thin silk of her dress. Bunching the fabric in his hands, he pulled her against him. "Why are you in a hurry? We have things to talk about."

"So talk! But first, let me go!" Sidonie squirmed, trying to get free. Her movements twisted her dress, causing both straps to slide down her arms.

Rafe looked down. Her dress had slipped down far enough that he could see her nipples. "I don't think I can. Damn it, Sidonie," he groaned. "Don't you ever wear underwear?"

She sucked in her breath, making the dress slip another inch or two. "All the time, including now!"

Now her breasts were almost completely exposed. "No bra. You didn't wear a bra. I might have known you'd wear something designed to drive a man crazy."

He couldn't resist. Rafe wrapped his hands tighter in the silk and tugged. The dress fell to her waist. Suddenly he couldn't think of one thing he had to say to her. He'd show her how he felt instead. With a satisfied grunt he lowered his head and took one hard pink pebble in his mouth.

"Rafe, wh-what are you— Oh!" As he suckled, she tangled her hands in his hair and pulled. "Stop…that! This minute, do you hear me?" He might have taken her at her word if she hadn't been pulling his head closer to her breasts. He obliged by switching his mouth to the other one.

"Rafe! I…said…stop." Her voice was so soft he could barely hear her over the pounding of his heart. "I don't want…"

He raised his head. "Yes, you do want. And so do I. I've wanted you from the first time I saw you. All evening long, when I was with Abby, I couldn't stop thinking about you. Whether you'd be at the dance. Who you'd be with. What you'd be wearing. Or not wearing."

She opened her mouth. Before she could argue with him more, he covered her mouth with his and showed her other uses for her sharp tongue.

He felt her knees start to buckle. Rafe leaned against the porch railing and let her fall against him. He slid his mouth down the curve of her jaw to the pulse beating frantically in her throat. His hands left the silk of her dress for the silk of her skin, moving to cover her breasts. Kneading gently, he nibbled on her earlobe, then returned to her mouth.

The kiss went on as long as he could breathe—hard, hot and needy. When he stopped, he was shaking and she was trembling.

"You taste like chocolate," she said, her soft mouth brushing his lips, her voice accusing.

"I had a piece of chocolate cake for supper."

"You had supper at Abby's." She tilted her head

back. "Did she make it from scratch? Silly question. Of course she did. Did she feed it to you?"

"No. I can feed myself. What's got you riled? Are you jealous?"

"Of course not." There it was again, that snooty look. "I was merely curious."

"Curiosity makes you snippy?"

"I am not snippy," she snapped. "Or, if I am, I have good reasons. I don't like being kidnapped." She scrubbed her mouth with the back of one hand, using the other to clutch her dress to her bosom. "And I hate being kissed."

"You do not. You like it when I kiss you." He kissed her again, to prove it. While she was clinging to him, he pushed open the front door and dragged her into the parlor.

He laid her on the sofa. She wrapped her arms around his neck and pulled him down on top of her.

What was he doing? Hadn't he decided a long time ago the kind of woman he wanted to marry? A woman like Cathy Sue—pretty but practical. Abby Hedgpeth should have been perfect. But she hadn't made his blood sing or his heart pound. Abby's chocolate cake had melted on his tongue, but he'd rather use his tongue to melt Sidonie.

He wanted Sidonie. Not only her gorgeous body… he wanted something else…. As soon as he could think again, he'd figure out what that something was.

Sidonie's heartbeat, already too fast, speeded up. Something too good to be true was happening, and she couldn't quite take it in. Rafe had fought over her, carried her away from the Spring Dance like a conquering hero, and now he was all but making love to her in the front parlor.

There was no reason for him to act so out of character, no reason at all, not unless...he loved her, too. Loved her enough that he'd forgotten all about his silly list of essential ingredients for a wife.

She tried to stop kissing him long enough to tell him she loved him, too, but he wouldn't let go of her mouth. Then, when he'd kissed and stroked her until they were both panting with need, he groaned, "Why can't you be like Abby?"

Sidonie stiff-armed him. He fell off her and the couch, ending up flat on his back on the floor.

"You rat," she said, sitting up and pulling her dress back into place.

"I didn't mean..." He raised himself up on his elbows, closing his eyes. "All I meant was, why can't you be the kind of woman who wants to settle down? Get married."

"Married? *Married?* Me?"

"I think it takes two. How about you and me?" He sat up and twisted around until he was more or less kneeling in front of her.

"Us get married? You are out of your mind. What about your essentials? I don't have a single one of them. Even if I did, I can't stay here. I have a job waiting in Fort Worth."

"A job? They offered you a job?"

"Don't act so surprised. I am good at what I do."

Rafe got up slowly and stood over her. "You'd rather dance in the chorus than marry me?" His voice was controlled, distant, but his eyes were bleak.

An anguished moan almost escaped her lips. She bit it back. "*You* don't want to marry *me*. You only think you do because you're tired of waiting for Miss Perfect to show up.'' She pushed an errant curl out of her face. ''Look, Rafe. I may or may not be ready to settle down. But I'll never be ready to be settled for.''

''I'm not settling—''

''Oh, no, of course not. I'm just perfect for you. You love my cooking and my choice of career, but there's one problem, Rafe. I have an essential, too. Only one. And you don't have it.''

''What is it?''

''If you have to ask—good night, Rafe.''

Sidonie gently closed the door to her room. She leaned against it until she heard Rafe's footsteps retreating down the hall to his room.

The next morning when she awoke, Gypsy was in her place at the foot of her bed. Jasmine and the kittens were curled up in a furry tangle on the pillow next to her head.

But Rafe was gone. Sometime during the night, he'd packed his bags and moved out.

Chapter Ten

The night of the long-awaited housewarming, Rafe walked through his house, showing it off to Cornelius Fielding. The pride, the sense of accomplishment he'd anticipated when he'd planned this moment was missing. He knew why, of course. He needed someone there to share the moment with, someone besides the guests who were slowly filling up all the open spaces. But the someone he wanted didn't want him.

"Well, where is she?" asked Cornelius as they returned to the living room.

"Who?"

"I've seen the land and the house. But as I recall there was a third component to your plan. The woman. Haven't you found her yet?"

"Oh, I found her."

"Introduce me."

"I can't. She's not here."

"Rafe, I always admired your succinct reports, but

you are taking terseness too far. Explain yourself, my boy.''

"It's a short story. I found her. I asked her to marry me. She turned me down. Emphatically."

"Ah. Emphatically. Interesting choice of words, that. I take it she wasn't—what was your requirement?—docile."

Rafe snorted. "Not at all." *Docile?* What had he been thinking of when he'd added that to his list? He didn't want a wimp for a wife. He wanted Sidonie, a passionate, teasing temptress.

"I never did understand your wanting that particular quality. I think a docile woman would bore you."

"Tell me about it." But by the time he'd figured that out, it was too late. Sidonie was on her way out of town, back to the life she adored. She couldn't wait to leave him in the dust.

"Who was she? Are you sure she's not here? It looks like the whole state is in your backyard."

"Sidonie Saddler. You passed her house on the way here."

"Sidonie? The woman you were living with? The chorus girl?"

"Dancer."

"Why did she turn you down?"

"She had a better offer. Dancing in the chorus at Casa Mañana this summer."

"Are you sure that's the reason?"

Rafe looked at Cornelius. He should have remembered Fielding would never accept an incomplete report. "She thought she didn't have what I wanted—those damned essentials. She said she wouldn't be settled for."

"I can understand that. After all your years of planning, deciding on the exact qualities you wanted in a woman—maybe she was right.''

"She was wrong. But I couldn't convince her. And now she's leaving town.''

"So it's over between you?''

"Yeah. She's going back to her career.''

"Are you going after her?''

"What for? She'd only turn me down again.''

"Would she?'' Cornelius gave Rafe a quizzical look. "We've known each other for fifteen years, but it didn't strike me until this minute just how much you've changed. When we first met, you were reckless and a little wild—luckily for me. A cautious man wouldn't have taken on three kidnappers and saved my life.''

"I was younger then. I had to learn sense sometime.''

"You got afraid, somewhere along the way. Afraid you wouldn't get your dream. That's why you never called it anything but a plan. When a plan fails, it's not a tragedy. Not like a dream that dies.''

"I might have gotten a little cautious over the years.''

"So you started holding something back—twenty percent, wasn't it?—to make sure you'd get what you wanted.''

"It worked.''

"You might have gotten your land sooner if you'd risked everything on one plunge in the market.''

"And I might have lost everything the same way. Doing things my way might have taken me longer, but I got what I wanted.''

"Not everything. What did you hold back from Sidonie?''

"Not a damn thing."

"Did you tell her you love her?"

"No." Rafe felt a jolt of recognition. *Love*. That was the something else he'd wanted. He wanted Sidonie to love him at least as much as she loved dancing. He stared at Cornelius.

"I think you held back your heart, Rafe. Because you were afraid to risk that much. But any woman worth having is not going to let you get away with that. If Sidonie's anything like my Mary was, she's going to want your heart and your soul forever."

Cornelius slapped Rafe on the back and walked away. "I've monopolized enough of your time. See to your other guests. I think I'll have a look around."

Sidonie sat on the porch swing, hoping its squeaky rocking would soothe her battered spirit. She'd watched as car after car had driven by on the way up the hill to Rafe's house. She'd seen Judge Longstreet go by in his vintage Cadillac, followed by Cathy Sue and J.D. in their Suburban. There had even been a mystery guest in a limousine with darkly tinted windows.

Jasmine jumped into her lap and began kneading her thigh. Absently Sidonie stroked the cat. Maybe she should have accepted Rafe's proposal. Taking advantage of a man's momentary lapse from sanity might not have been such a bad thing. At least she wouldn't feel as if her heart had been ripped from her chest, leaving a big, empty hole.

But how long would it have been before Rafe realized he'd made a mistake? Maybe only days. The man had known what kind of woman he wanted to marry for fifteen years, and it sure wasn't anyone remotely like her. And she couldn't change, not for a man who didn't know there was only one essential ingredient needed for a lifelong partnership.

Love.

Rafe had never said he loved her. Love wasn't even on his list. A tear trickled down her cheek, and she angrily brushed it away.

A car stopped at the end of her walk. Maggie Parker rolled down the passenger window. "Want a ride?" she called.

"No, thanks. I'm not going."

Maggie was out of the car and on the front porch in a flash. "What do you mean you're not going? Everyone in town is going. Except for Abby and Bobby Lee. They eloped."

"Did they?"

"So the field is clear, so to speak. And I don't think Cathy Sue will be doing any more matchmaking. She finally failed at something. Isn't that great?"

"Great."

"Show a little enthusiasm, Sidonie. And get dressed. We'll wait."

"I'm still not going. I have to pack."

Maggie put her hands on her hips and glared at Sidonie. "So you're giving up. You're just going to pack your bag and sneak out of town without saying goodbye to anyone. I'm ashamed of you, Sidonie Saddler. I thought you had spunk."

"I'm not wasting spunk on a skunk."

"Rafe's not a skunk. He's confused. Men get that way when they fall in love."

"He's not in love with me. And he never will be. I'm not who he wants."

"Who else?"

"The hedgehog, or someone like her. Come to think of it, a hedgehog and a skunk make a perfect pair."

"You'd do that to him? Let him make the mistake of his life?"

"I'm the mistake he would have made if I'd let him. He has a list, Maggie, a list of six essential qualities for a wife. I don't have any of them."

"Not one?"

"Well, maybe one. *Attractive.*"

"You've got that one, all right, in spades. And you must have others, too. How about *smart, sassy* and *sexy?*"

"Not on the list."

Rolling her eyes, Maggie sat down next to Sidonie and gave the swing a push. "Then the man is deluding himself. Trust me. All men want *sexy.* And they get used to *smart* and *sassy.* Eventually." She waved at Rayburn, waiting patiently in the car.

"Oh, Rafe wants me. Or he did. But he doesn't love me."

"How do you know? Have you asked him?"

"No. I shouldn't have to ask."

"Go to the party, Sidonie. If he loves you, give him the chance to tell you so. If he doesn't, at least give him—and the town—something to remember you by."

With that parting shot, Maggie walked briskly back to her car and the Parkers drove away, up the hill to Rafe's house.

Sidonie felt her heart begin to beat faster. Maggie had been right. Not about Rafe. He didn't love her. But about her. Why should she creep out of town like a whipped puppy? If her years onstage had taught her anything, it was how to make an exit.

She leapt out of the swing and headed for her bedroom.

Opening the closet, she surveyed her choices. Choice. She only had the slip dress she'd worn to the Spring Dance. True, it had started a fight, but she wanted something different, something...outrageous. With a grin, Sidonie reached for a costume Belle had made for her years ago.

At the top of the hill, Sidonie managed to squeeze her truck between a Mercedes-Benz and an oak tree. She got out, smoothed her dress into place and walked to the house. The front door was open, and some people were standing on the wide veranda. Sidonie walked through the door and looked around. A few people were touring the house—she saw Elise herding a group up the curved staircase—but most of the activity seemed to be out back, around the barbecue pit and the swimming pool. She went outside.

A band, steel guitars, a keyboard and drums, was set up on a small stage at one end of the pool. Some people were dancing, others were lined up at a long buffet table, loading plates with barbecue, potato salad and other goodies. She saw Maggie and Rayburn sitting poolside on lounge chairs, deep in conversation with Judge Longstreet.

"Good grief, everyone in the county must be here," she muttered, worming her way through the crowd. But Rafe was nowhere in sight.

"My, my. I'm surprised to see you here."

Sidonie glanced over her shoulder. "Hello, Cathy Sue. J.D."

Cathy Sue, wearing a designer cotton dress, looked Sidonie over from head to toe. Smiling, she said,

"Aren't you a little overdressed for a simple country barbecue?"

"Probably," Sidonie agreed. She was wearing a blue velvet cape over a blue satin gown. "But don't let it spoil your evening. I won't be for long."

"Excuse me?" said Cathy Sue, a puzzled look on her flawless face.

"Never mind. Have you seen Rafe?"

"Not lately." Cathy Sue took her by the arm. "Don't go, Sidonie. I want to talk to you. If you decide to stay in town, I'd like to trade cooking lessons for Darcy's dance lessons."

That got her attention. "You'd teach me how to cook?"

"Yes. I'm a pretty fair country cook. Ask anyone."

"I've heard. But why?"

Cathy Sue blushed. "I'm sorry I interfered with you and Rafe. Abby Hedgpeth wasn't right for him. I should have seen that."

"There is no me and Rafe, but thanks." Sidonie patted Cathy Sue on the hand. "Thanks for the offer of cooking lessons, too. If I were going to hang around, I'd definitely take you up on it. Now, would you excuse me? I've got something to do."

Sidonie left Cathy Sue and made her way through the crush to the bandstand.

"Hello, pretty lady. Any requests?" asked the bandleader.

She gave him a brilliant smile. "As a matter of fact, I have a very special request. Do you know..." Sidonie stood on tiptoe and whispered in the bandleader's ear.

With a chuckle he nodded and helped her onto the

stage. As he told the other band members what Sidonie had requested, she took the mike.

"Good evening, ladies and gentlemen. For those of you who don't know me, I'm Sidonie Saddler, and I'm going to dance for you this evening. My farewell to Cache, you might say."

The bandleader provided a drumroll, and people began gathering in front of the stage.

"I'm sure you've all heard the tale of how our host left town fifteen years ago. Remember? He ran off with an exotic dancer, or so the story goes. Personally I don't think it's true. But in honor of myths, and for auld lang syne—"

Another drumroll sounded, and the band began to play a raunchy bump-and-grind song. Facing the crowd, Sidonie untied the cape and began slipping it off, first baring one shoulder, then the other. At a crescendo of steel guitars, she let the cape slide completely off, revealing the costume she'd last worn when trying out for a part in *Gypsy*. She was wearing a long blue satin dress with white kid gloves.

The drummer picked up the beat, and Sidonie followed his lead, undulating across the stage, swinging her hips from side to side in time with the music. She slid the skirt of her dress up, revealing a long length of leg clad in black silk stockings.

As a few catcalls sounded from the rowdier guests, Sidonie swayed seductively and slowly stripped off one of the long kid gloves she wore. When she'd gotten it off, she twirled it over her head, then tossed it into the audience.

A few more bumps and grinds, and Sidonie started on the second glove. She'd just worked it off when she saw the crowd parting. Rafe McMasters was headed for the stage, and he didn't look happy.

Sidonie tossed the second glove into the crowd in front of Rafe. Several men jumped for it, momentarily blocking Rafe's path to the stage.

Quickly Sidonie found the zipper at the back of the dress and tugged. The blue satin began sliding seductively down her body. Before it reached her waist, Rafe was next to her.

"What in hell are you doing?" He snagged the blue dress and pulled it up over the low-cut, glimmering bodysuit covering her body.

"Dancing. Let me go and get off the stage. You're in my way."

"Tough." He held her dress in place with one hand and reached for the microphone with the other. "Entertainment's over, folks."

Rafe lifted her off the stage and, holding her back against him, marched her through the crowd and into the house. He didn't stop until they were in the master bedroom.

"What possessed you to pull a stunt like that?" He let go of her, and the dress started its slide down her body again.

She grabbed it and turned her back to him. "Zip me up, please."

As he fumbled with the zipper, Sidonie took a deep breath. Now or never, she told herself. Closing her eyes, she said, "Rafe? I have a question for you."

"What is it?"

"Do you love me?"

Silence. She looked at him over her shoulder. Rafe stared at her, obviously stunned. He didn't say one word.

Sidonie jerked away from him and ran.

* * *

As soon as she was home, she raced to the bedroom and pulled her suitcase from the closet shelf. She had to keep moving, faster and faster. If she stopped the pain might catch up with her. She began tossing clothes into the suitcase, willy-nilly.

"Smart, sassy and sexy, huh? How about stupid, stupid and stupid? I've never been so humiliated in my whole life."

She threw the last of her clothes into the suitcase and tried to shut it. It wouldn't close.

"Idiot. You know how to pack." She dumped the contents on the bed and started over. This time she slowed down, folding each piece carefully.

As she worked, Gypsy came and sat at her feet. Jasmine twined herself in and out between her ankles. As she repacked the suitcase, she talked to them.

"I never should have listened to Maggie. She was wrong. Rafe doesn't love me. Come to think of it, I probably don't love him, either. When you love someone, you want them to be happy. Personally, I hope he's miserable for the rest of his life."

The two kittens climbed up the bedspread and curled up in the suitcase.

"Oh, no," whispered Sidonie, miserably. "My life doesn't fit in a suitcase anymore."

"It doesn't matter. I've got plenty of room—for you and your menagerie."

Sidonie whirled around. "Rafe! What are you doing here?"

"I came to answer your question."

Her chin came up. "You already did. Silence speaks volumes."

"You rendered me speechless. And about the time

I got my voice back, you'd run away. It took me a while to get here because everyone wanted to know when you were coming back to finish the show.''

"I'm not.''

"Darn right, you're not. No wife of mine is stripping in public. Privately, just between the two of us, is another matter." He handed her the white kid gloves she'd worn. "You'll need these. For later."

Taking the gloves, Sidonie stared at him, her heart beating painfully. "W-wife? Me?"

"Who else?"

"What about your six essentials?"

"You've always had the important ones. You were born in Cache. You're attractive."

"I'm not a homemaker."

"I've never felt so at home in my life as I did the weeks we lived together. You sure made this old house a home."

"Homemakers can cook. I can't."

"I like your cooking."

She raised an eyebrow. "Oh, really?"

"Yes, really," he mimicked. "It's different. Spontaneous. Unpredictable. Spicy. Just like you."

She didn't believe him for a minute. But he didn't know Cathy Sue was going to give her cooking lessons. She could handle that essential, with a little help from her friends. But there were others.

"Maternal—you want someone who's maternal and I've never even been around children, except the kind with stage mothers."

"You make a pet out of every animal you come across—that's maternal."

"Well, I'm not respectable."

"You know what I think? I think you only pretend

to be wicked to shock fuddy-duddies and stuffed shirts.''

"How about docile? I've never been docile in my life. And I never will be.''

"That's true, but it's okay. I've revised my list. The only real essential is that I love you and you love me. Do you? Or did you mean it when you said you wanted me to be miserable for the rest of my life?''

"Yes."

"You want me to be miserable?''

"No. I meant 'Yes, I love you.'"

"And you'll be a rancher's wife?''

"Looks that way."

After a few delicious kisses, Sidonie sighed. "Can I name all our cows?''

"Absolutely not."

"Oh. Well then, about those potbellied pigs..."

"No. Not on your life. I am not going to be a pig farmer's husband.''

"But, Rafe. They're so cute and cuddly.''

"So am I. Concentrate on cuddling me, why don't you?''

"Not a bad idea, cowboy.''

Epilogue

Sidonie and Cornelius Fielding stood at the top of the curving staircase, waiting for Belle to begin playing the wedding march on the new baby grand piano. Sidonie was wearing a full-length white lace wedding gown, with long sleeves and a high neck, and a full set of underwear. Rafe had chosen her wardrobe.

Maggie Parker, Sidonie's matron of honor, was standing a few steps below them. She was dressed in pale pink satin. Sidonie would have chosen a brighter pink, but she hadn't been consulted.

"Did I thank you for the piano?" whispered Sidonie.

"Three or four times."

"It was very nice of you, but a baby grand was just a bit extravagant, don't you think? An upright would have been fine. You know, Corny, just because you're a multibillionaire doesn't mean you should throw your money around. Do you have a financial plan? Plans are very important—"

"Good grief, you sound like Rafe and you're not even married yet."

Sidonie grinned. "You didn't let me finish. Plans are important, because interfering with them is so much fun."

"Uh-oh. What have you done now?"

"Wait and see."

The music started, and Maggie began a slow walk down the stairs. Sidonie drifted gracefully after her on Cornelius's arm. Rafe stood waiting in front of the marble fireplace with his best man, Dr. Parker.

Judge Longstreet performed the ceremony in record time, and the wedding party moved to the waiting cars. Rafe had planned a small family wedding at home, followed by a reception for the whole town at the Proffit County Grange Hall.

"I'll drive," said Sidonie, ignoring Corny's limousine and heading for her red pickup truck. She'd left the keys in the ignition.

Bemused, Rafe followed and climbed into the passenger seat. "Decided you're going to be the boss in this family, hmm?"

"Was that bossy?" She winked at him. "I'm sorry."

Once they got to town, Sidonie drove right by the Grange Hall and turned her pickup onto Highway 283.

"Where are you going? Our reception's back there."

"We're not going to our reception. Not just yet."

"What do you mean, we're not going? The reception's been planned for weeks. We can't just leave town, Sidonie. And there's no reason to drive to Dallas. You know Corny's jet is waiting for us at the Proffit County Airport."

"Yes, I know. It was clearly stated in your written plan for our wedding." Sidonie smiled at him, but she didn't turn the pickup around. "It was really sweet of you to plan the wedding and the reception and the honeymoon."

"Well, someone had to do it, and you didn't have time. You had to finish your job at Casa Mañana. Besides, I'm good at planning."

"Yes, dear."

"Now turn around and go back to town."

"No, dear. Not yet." She pulled into the drive of the Mustang Motel, parking the truck in front of room six. "There's something we have to do first." She dipped a hand down the front of her dress and fished out a key.

"Sidonie—"

"Rafe, your plan for our wedding was great, but it had one big flaw."

His brown eyes narrowed. "Oh, yeah, and what was that?"

"You scheduled the wedding for noon, the reception from one to three, followed immediately by a quick trip to Dallas on Corny's jet, then an eight-hour flight to Paris. Don't you see? You left out something very important."

"What?"

"Oh, for heaven's sake." She unlocked the door and stepped into the motel room. "Our wedding night."

Rafe followed her into the room. A bottle of champagne was chilling in a plastic ice bucket, and something hot pink and filmy was draped on the turned-down covers of the bed.

"I planned a wedding night," Rafe said. "At the Georges Cinq—I reserved the honeymoon suite."

"Yes, I know, and I'm sure it will be lovely. But by the time we land in Paris, go through customs, get to the hotel, it will be tomorrow night—and that's not counting the difference in time. I want my wedding night tonight. Or this afternoon, whichever comes first."

Rafe drew his brows together in a frown. "Sidonie, everyone knows your red pickup. If we spend the afternoon at this tacky motel, by the time we get back to the Grange Hall, the whole town will know what we've been doing. We'll be the talk of Proffit County for years."

"What's your point?" She untied his tie, then began removing the studs from his tuxedo shirt.

"I don't remember." Rafe wrapped his arms around his wife and began working loose the dozen covered buttons on her wedding dress.

"Well then, as we say in show business, let's get this show on the road."

* * * * *